THE IDEA MAN

A Novel of Adventure, Friendship, and the Secret of Life

by

JOSH GREEN

Illustrated by

KRYSTAL TAVARES

Lō'ihi Press
Honolulu

www.loihipress.com

FIRST EDITION

ISBN-13: 978-0-9822535-1-9

Lō'ihi Press
733 Bishop Street
Suite 2302
Honolulu, Hawai'i 96813
www.loihipress.com

For my family and all my dearest friends

Contents

1. Meet Plum

Hello, my name is Boy. Yes it's an odd name. Blame my parents if it bothers you, but know from the start that this isn't a story about me. It's about a person named Larry Plum and the adventures we had together.

Larry Plum lost his middle name and was forever in search of it. Plum, my best friend for an entire lifetime, or two as he sometimes said, was an idea man, and his ideas took us to the far reaches of the world. "This world is a wonderful place," he said, "and it is really no wonder at all that the Seven Wonders of the World were built on ideas! Only really there are eight."

I met Plum when we were a hair short of six years old. I had just moved into his town, Seasoncreek, and because school was out, my parents sent me off to the local baseball field so that I could meet other kids. I was very anxious—and not just because I had no friends yet. I was also a weak baseball player, and this was the last thing that I wanted an intimidating bunch of five- six- and seven-year-olds to know about me first.

I was actually a passable fielder, with a half-decent arm and a flare for the dramatic catch. But I couldn't hit the ball a lick, and there's nothing like a strikeout to put the new kid on the bench for the summer, and maybe a lifetime.

I prayed to be sent to the outfield and amazingly the call came.

"New kid, come here," I heard from deep centerfield. "I need help!"

I was blinded for a second, as I stared into a blast of early July sun. All I could make out was the figure of a boy, roughly my dimensions, but with a head that seemed a little too big for a body that size.

"Hurry up, new kid! Help me get this infernal thing off. It's smushing my skull, and I can't stand it another second!"

I trotted up to the boy who was frantically trying to extract his slightly oversized head from a well worn, dusty black-and-gold Pittsburgh Pirates baseball cap. He was clutching and yanking at the hat, as if it had a demonic suction hold on him.

"Grab it and help me off with this mean thing!" he said. "It's squeezing my brains down into my body. Don't be shy. Just get a hold and pull!"

I grabbed hold with both hands and leaned backwards, expecting the cap to come off easily (after all, it was only a baseball cap). It didn't. I gave a more deliberate yank while he leaned the opposite way. Wouldn't budge. Then I tried screwing it off, like the lid on a pickle jar. It rotated a bit, but didn't pop off. Before I knew it, we were both on the ground, me with my feet set against his shoulders, applying leverage to hat and boy.

"That's it, now really give it a go," Plum yelled. "Use those new kid legs of yours, and we'll have it!"

2

I pushed with my legs, and he pulled. I was as determined as a boy aiming to get into a forbidden cookie jar left accidentally within reach. Plum strained again and I gave one final pull with all my five-year-old might. I heard his neck crack like knuckles, then off flew that "infernal" Pirates cap, and me too, rolling three somersaults backwards and finishing up with a cartwheel to the side.

When I got to my feet, I saw him cap in hand, examining it like a stamp collector might examine rare postage, or a mathematician some new proof.

"Just as I suspected," Plum said. "It's no smaller than it was before. It's my head that's grown."

Now he looked at me directly.

"You know, a person's head grows exactly two sizes bigger when an idea of any importance comes into it! There's no getting around that. I'm through with hats. Who ever saw a thinking person with a hat on his head? And thank you for removing mine!"

This was my first experience with Larry Plum, an Idea Man even as a boy. We were best friends from that day forward—like twin brothers, without the dangers of common blood to complicate our friendship. To my recollection, Plum never did wear another hat. Not to the end of his days—and they were exceptionally many. And it's a good thing too, because on many occasions a hat would have been the end of him.

2. Joe's Giant Gumball Machine

When I met Larry Plum, I believed like most five-year-olds that life is simple and things happen for a reason. Plum had a different idea. Before he'd turned six, Plum seemed to have the insight of a wise adult. His thoughts on issues foremost in the minds of other very young males—from time travel to hair loss—stimulated my own curiosity and focused my developing brain. Why Plum had wisdom on such subjects at age six, I can't say—and neither could he. He could only tell me that his ideas "just popped in there."

Plum's ideas didn't come from our formal education. We were in second grade at the Be Kind Elementary School (the BKE), a progressive but hardly awe-inspiring program. Travel hadn't expanded Plum's mind either. He had only recently gotten permission to cross the street by himself, and even this privilege had limitations. So the question remained: where did Larry Plum's ideas come from? Above or worse yet, below, I supposed.

On our way to and from school every day we passed Joe's general store. It was really more of a market than a store, loaves of bread and orange juice at premium prices. Most important to me, Joe's store had lots of candy. But candy didn't interest Plum much at that age, until The Machine landed.

We got out of school late that day because of a comment I had made about our principal's *lack of a sense of humor*. Delayed freedom, and our general distaste for the elementary school's penal system, had us running fast and late for the ball field, passing Joe's on our right. Four steps past Joe's door, I realized I was alone.

I looked back, and saw Plum with his face pressed close to Joe's store window, nostrils flaring, fogging up the glass.

"What is it, Plum?"

He turned, looked at me hard, then turned back to Joe's window. This made me rant a bit.

"Come on, we're late for the game!" He didn't even turn his head, as he stepped into the store. I looked down at my feet, at the sky above, then all around. I took two steps towards the baseball field, then turned six steps back, and followed Plum in.

Plum was face to face with The Beast—the biggest, most colorful, globular, gumball machine of our time. Of any time!

"Can you see it?" Plum said.

"What do you mean? What do you want me to see?"

The Machine was seven feet tall, with a globe no less than four feet across. It was filled with what seemed like millions of gumballs. There were twelve colors—ten, if you subscribe to the lunacy that white and black aren't colors. Purple, yellow, red, orange, green, blue, pink, aqua, white,

The Idea Man

black, maroon, and a neon color that can only really be described as "bright gum." The gumballs were thrown together in ways that made your eyes whirl and brain twist. Green against orange over yellow, forever far from black, then a swath of maroon cutting though pink, aqua, and neon. Plum was looking so deeply into The Machine's innards that it's a wonder he didn't seize up.

"Can you see it?" Plum whispered. "Can you see it?"

His eyes were really wide, pupils dilated to the full, swallowing light in gulps, not sips.

"I see gum, Plum!" I said quietly, pleased that I had rhymed.

"No!"

He walked out—down the street, around the corner, and out of sight. I saw gum. Plum clearly saw something else all together.

The next morning, a Saturday in fact, I put on the clothes that had fallen nearest to my bed the previous week. Before she could complete her speech on the merits of a good breakfast before a long day of work or play, I passed my mother, and was out the laundry room door.

"Goodbye, sweetheart. Call if you go someplace strange, and be home for lunch or dinner, whichever comes first."

Mother was my loving caretaker, who knew the value of Saturday freedom to a boy. Dad was also great, but lived the life of a weekend chore-warrior—already mowing, raking, or stacking bricks somewhere on the property. If I didn't make eye contact, I had a chance at the carefree day with Plum that I had dreamt about the night before. Eye contact was fatal.

"Boy, come here and help me for one minute!"

Three hours and fourteen minutes later, I was at Plum's door. Don't feel sorry for me, it wasn't ten yet, and Plum was a late riser unless I called, so I probably hadn't missed much. And besides, I had that curious sense of accomplishment one gets after moving nine hundred and forty-two bricks from one perfectly good pile to another. Thanks, Dad.

I walked into the Plum's sunroom without a knock, ring, or bang. The Plums and I were close enough to dispense with the usual pleasantries.

"Where is Plum, Mrs. Plum?"

"He's gone, Boy. Left through the basement door a few minutes ago."

"Did he go through the Rogers' yard?"

"Probably. I don't know. He said he would be back, but that's all."

I headed for the door with no important information.

"Wait up, Boy, have some breakfast. I cooked all of this . . ."

I slipped four English muffins and two handfuls of bacon into my knapsack for Plum and myself.

"OK, thanks, goodbye."

I was through the door before she finished her morning menu. If I had looked back, which I certainly didn't do—never look back!—I would have seen her smile. She approved of me.

I passed underneath the oak where Plum had his two front teeth extracted the week before—a climbing-falling incident. Passing through the Roger's yard—"Go around, Boy!" Mrs. Rogers yelled—and I headed for The Machine.

Joe's store opened at ten. I was there one minute after, breathing hard. Plum had only just arrived himself, thirty seconds ahead of me. This must have shocked Joe.

The Idea Man

We were never the first to arrive anywhere. Plum always paced himself, arriving in his own good time. But on that day we were at Joe's hours before his usual clientele rolled in for their expensive bread and juice.

"Boy! What brings you here so early? Has your mother burned the last of your bacon, or are you short on syrup for the family pancakes?"

Joe was crotchety with a saucy bite.

"No. I believe we're here to explore this gumball machine," I said, looking at Plum. I handed Joe a ten-dollar bill and two ones that Plum had just shoved into my hand. He didn't like to talk to Joe.

"Please change this to nickels for me. And no dimes! They don't fit."

Ordinarily, Joe would have sent us packing with an earful. But now he had The Machine and our money, and returned from the back several minutes later with the two hundred and forty nickels Plum wanted. "Thank you. This silver will prove most helpful, I'm sure." And we set to it.

Within minutes, a flood of gum was streaming from The Machine into Plum's pockets, which bulged like Mr. Sicily's belly after Mrs. Sicily had fed him his standard "three plates of pasta and balls." Or like Mrs. Sicily's own belly, before she delivered triplets on the hottest day ever recorded in Seasoncreek—one hundred and six degrees Fahrenheit! Soon Plum's pockets were completely full.

"Boy, come closer. I need help!" I sidled up to him, standing in the shadow of the massive gumball machine, and he began unloading gumballs into my knapsack

I was shocked. Plum didn't even chew gum. But my pack was half full, and Plum's money was gone, before I had the courage to ask the all-important question that I now know the world revolves around.

8

"Why?"

"Why, Boy? Why hundreds and hundreds of purple, red, orange, green, white, and blue gumballs? Because they're random. They keep coming, wave after wave, but never like five minutes ago."

"So what, Plum? You hate gum, but you've cornered the market."

Plum then pointed to his notebook, which I hadn't noticed before. Inside, he'd swiftly written the following:

The Idea Man

Page after page of colors, recording the order that the gumballs had passed from The Machine into Plum's hands, past his mouth, and into his pockets and my bag. Patterns that never repeated, never resembled one another.

"Don't you see Boy? It's never the same, never even close. Just like people, Boy. They never come out the same, they never will. The random nature of the universe is at work here in Joe's Giant Gumball Machine!"

Then Plum walked out of Joe's store, without another word to me, or a gumball in hand.

And at age five, I knew. Nothing ever does come out the same—and that's a secret to life.

3. Harvest

There is no season to match the spring, when the earth explodes, gardens roar, and the flowers take control. There's something in the liberation from winter that can lift any spirit, even a cynical one, so when that first spring breeze hits the nostrils and the buds emerge, watch out! My first spring in Seasoncreek was one to remember. Plum made sure of that. But this story begins the previous August, when Plum and I were six years old.

School was about to start, and we were getting in our last licks at the summer. That August was a scorcher, and normally we would have gone swimming at Meadow Pond, about a mile from home. But Plum had seen a big snake there the day before, so we were a bit wary. Instead we decided to run the sprinklers of Seasoncreek. Our town was full of what Plum called "obsessive gardeners." No lawn was too green, and no flowerbed was too neat, so all of their sprinkler systems were on full throttle.

Our game was a simple one. We ran from yard to yard, trying for the maximum soak a boy with pruning skin could get without being caught. Meanwhile, the frustrated gardeners tried to spy on us so that they could inform our parents about the evils of unbridled children. For the garden prudes, our trespasses seemed like matters of life and death, though "Nothing ever is unless you're actually dying," as Plum pointed out. For us, though, it was a boyhood adventure—until the Seasoncreek Garden Club sprung its trap.

It seems that Plum and I had worn out our garden tour welcome earlier that summer. Several members of the Club's secret society convened an emergency meeting to address the problem of two wreck-loose boys tromping through their over-pruned hedges. At first they posted community lookouts to try and stop us. But as seasoned marauders, we never took the same route twice, so their watch, based on patterns they thought we followed, failed. Then they got smarter, and hired a tail.

Early one Sunday, we were out exploring Seasoncreek, looking for an adventure. Most of "the watch" was in church so we thought we were safe. Then Plum stopped me in my tracks.

"We've been made, Boy," he whispered.

"No way, Plum. You know they're off praying, or whatever it is they do. It's Sunday."

"No, Boy. It's much too quiet."

Now paranoid, we changed course and made it as far as the Wilsons' yard two blocks away. We had just cleared the hedge when suddenly the Wilsons' crazy Doberman Pincer, always leashed in the past, sprang! I slipped just as it leapt, clearing me by six inches. Plum yanked me to my feet, and pushed me to the picket fence at the back of the property. There was a loosened fence plank, courtesy of a claw hammer and Plum's forethought. We were through the fence like mongooses—mongeese?—but not before that Pincer had pinced my right buttock.

I yelped, and we ran hard and fast down Mitchell Lane, then threw ourselves under a holly bush to catch our breath.

"How did that dog get unleash—"

And then I saw him, tearing down the street after us.

Now we were really moving. The next garden was Professor Hammond's, an old and nasty organic chemist who was already after us for us experimenting with his discarded chemicals the week before. We scrambled over his fence and dropped into his yard, safe from the Doberman—but now the hot breath of Hammond's bulldog was in my face. From the corner of my eye, I saw the mad scientist on his porch, holding a loose leash. We were in big trouble—two boys, two dogs, and fewer options every second.

After Hammond's, the rest was a blur. One yard after another brought a new dog and a new bruise or wound. This made us suspicious. Some of these people didn't even own dogs, but they had them that Sunday morning. After an eternity of fences, gates, and canine incisors, we found ourselves at the edge of Mary Roberts Reinhart Park, home to the Meadow Pond that could have saved us this cannonball run in the first place if it hadn't been for that random snake spotting!

The Idea Man

Dogs or snake, snake or dogs? Snake! So we dove headfirst into the deep warm water, where no fool dog would follow. When we surfaced, Plum took my arm and turned me toward the shore so that I could see our company. Every Garden Club member was there, and so was the Minister they had convinced to postpone the 10 a.m. service for the sake of revenge. He also had a spectacular sprinkler system that we never ignored.

The boy they'd hired to tail us was Murray, Plum's nemesis, who'd tracked us from yard to yard, so that every card-carrying Garden Club member and long-toothed pet knew we were coming. Someday, Murray would be dealt with. But first, the Garden Club. They would pay—I could see it in Plum's eyes.

My pride and my behind healed in a few days, and I had almost managed to forget the whole thing when Plum climbed through my third-story bedroom window like a shadow at 3 a.m.

"Boy, get up. I need your help."

I actually was up, sorting through my collection of baseball cards—men I worshipped who had retired years before I was born. Strange whom we idolize.

"I'm not going out there, if that's what you mean by help."

"It's revenge time, Boy, and we're a team."

"Revenge? Murray?"

"No. The gardeners. They need a lesson, and we're the ones to give it!"

Plum's justice streak ran very deep. For him life had a symmetry that had to be served. If people had a laugh at your expense, then you owed them one at theirs. He prodded me for a long time to go with him, but I was stubborn that night, and ultimately refused. So well before dawn he set out alone, slipping out my window, and clambering down the gutter to the ground. I saw him pick up a burlap sack and a hand shovel.

"See you in the morning, Boy."

He didn't look back, but waved over his head, then blended back into the shadows of the night.

The next day began messily. Torrential rains, rare in Seasoncreek, dumped a foot of water on us, and I was ordered to stay in and clean my room until all hours of the afternoon. It wasn't a small job, but I managed to clear my loose toys and clothing from the floor, packing everything so tightly under my bed that the mattress was lifted half an inch off of its frame. Proper sheet placement obscured the view, and I managed to pass inspection. Luckily. Mother always looked under my bed, but Dad usually stuck to a fly-by inspection from the doorway. He was in command that day. But then—

"Boy, how about coming to the office with me to do some collating?"

"Thanks, Dad, but I have plans, really. I should be going now."

Two hours, four minutes and seventy-six annual reports later—one hundred and ninety-nine pages in perfect table-of-contents-body-bibliography-acknowledgments order—Dad let me go.

"Thanks for your help, Boy. These reports are stunning. I couldn't have done it without you," he said with the wry, proud smirk of a father who had just helped his son to some healthy discipline.

I bolted to Plum's house. On the doorstep I saw his sneakers, caked with mud and dripping wet. Plum's sock footprints led me through the family room and up the stairs toward the bedroom. I followed the damp trail. His wet socks lay in a pile at his door, forming a dirty puddle.

The Idea Man

"What did you do, Plum?" The suspense was killing me. "What was in the burlap sack, and what was the shovel for, and—"

Plum smiled, then sneezed. I tossed a towel to him, hoping it would untie his tongue. It didn't.

"Come on! Just because I didn't go doesn't mean we're not a team. Plum, I'm sorry! I promise I'll go next time. Just tell me what you did."

My pleading got the better of him. He told me I was pathetic, but he decided to take pity on me.

So like I was saying, there's no season to match the spring, when the world grows green, gardens roar, and the earth explodes. That spring was a wet one, perfect for weeds of every variety. But no one expected what Seasoncreek had to offer by April. At the time when the garden elite had their noses highest in the air, looking down on the "natural" gardens of the community's "lay-gardeners," peculiar stocks began to erupt everywhere the eye wandered.

The Wilsons' garden was the first, followed by Hammond's, though the minister's probably got it worst. Tall, rapid-fire green asparagi were shooting up among the daffodils and daylilies of all the best gardens. Larry Plum had done some very special planting, and not a Garden Club plot was spared.

Thanks in large part to the lifetime supply of fertilizer that the Garden Club had poured onto their gardens, Seasoncreek was awash in the heartiest asparagus crop in its history. And no matter what the garden snobs tried, they were helpless. The more they pared the asparagus back, the thicker it returned. If they dared spray the vegetable, their pansies wilted, and if they ignored the asparagus, it took over completely. A plague had come, and all they could do was serve it with meatloaf.

I had never seen Plum happier. He complemented every gardener he saw on their banner asparagus crop, assuring each of them that it would only get better next season, because asparagus has the natural proclivity to spread its roots. Gardeners fumed countywide, while those who were spared the vegetable thanked themselves for having the good sense not to become overly proud of their natural gardens—or to set their dogs on us.

"Pride is a disease, after all," Plum said, "and asparagus is the cure."

"But what if they retaliate, Plum? What will you do?"

"They won't retaliate, Boy."

"How do you know? How can you be sure?"

"Because every Seasoncreek gardener knows that just as day follows night, eggplant follows asparagus."

There was no revenge. And Seasoncreek became the asparagus capital of the world.

4. On Time

"Being on time is very important to people Boy," Plum said to me one afternoon as we lay underneath the knobby oak at the corner of Pine and Mitchell, pulling up clumps of grass with our eight-year-old hands, and releasing them into the summer breeze. "And anyone who tells you to be on time more than once a day has some problem or another, probably psychological."

"Why Plum? Why is time so important?"

"Because there's not too much of it to go around."

And with that we set back to daydreaming. The air was warm, but the breeze was a cool blanket. I watched Plum as he slid in and out of sleep, and I thought about what he'd said. I always did seem to be late—most people said so anyhow. Did they all have psychological problems? I was really wondering about what Plum would say to that, so I woke him from a snoring summer nap by bouncing small stones off of his forehead.

"What? Why did you have to wake me up, Boy? I was just about to figure out something really important!"

"What was it?" I asked, somewhat guiltily.

"Darned it if I know, but it was something big!"

"I'm sorry, Plum. I only wanted to hear more about time, that's all."

"What about time, Boy? What did you want to know?" The sleep haze was still on him, and his lids began to droop.

"You know. About being on it."

He yawned. "Being on whaaattt? Whhhaaaaattt aaarrree youuuu tallllkking abooouuuuuuttttttt?" Sleep sent him reeling, and he started to snore again.

"Being on time, Plum, for God's sake!" My voice boomed. He sat straight up, eyes wide open.

"OK! Right! I remember now. Yes! In fact, that's just what I was dreaming about. Thank you for rousing me. It will be best to work this out awake. The best I can tell," he continued, "is that most people are constantly worrying that their time is running out. That's their problem. That's their mistake. Actually, time runs every direction but out. Time runs forward, backward, around in circles especially, but never out. We run out, Boy, not time."

I was a bit dumbfounded, but Plum seemed to know what he was talking about. So I kept quiet.

"The interesting thing, Boy, is that most people let time run their lives. It controls and stupefies them. *Time's running out! Where has all the time gone?* Or worst of all, *time is money!* Fools! We control time, Boy! It's ours!"

Then he fell back into the Plum dream world.

For me, this was a sudden awakening. I controlled time. It was mine. Who would have dreamt such a thing? So I set off on a walk. Plum had provided the theory. Now it needed a measure of practical application.

Since I was always considered late, I thought first about making days longer. I tried a thirty-hour-day out in my head, but the sun kept setting too early or too late, and I was still getting hungry on a regular schedule. No, the day needed to remain twenty-four-hours long.

Hours and minutes came under scrutiny next.

At first a ninety-second-minute seemed just right. "Give me a minute," now actually meant something (try it out, you'll feel less rushed). So I spent most of that afternoon getting a feel for a life made up of ninety-second-minutes. It was going quite well—until I realized how fast the hours seemed to go by. My God, it seemed like an hour passed every forty minutes! I couldn't have that, and certainly not during the summer!

I then tried seventy-five-minute-hours with the original sixty-second-minutes, and was fairly comfortable with them, until I realized that none of the numbers worked out on clocks. The hour wasn't easily divisible; even half an hour was entirely too complicated. I spent that day confused, wandering miles and miles for forty, fifty-five, seventy-five and ninety-minute hours. When I finally settled on one-hundred-twenty-minute-hours filled with thirty-second-minutes, I found myself back where I had started—at the corner of Pine and Mitchell. Plum was still asleep beneath the oak tree.

"Plum! Wake up! I think I'm onto something."

Plum's right eye opened half a crack and focused. I had awakened him twice now. "Yes, Boy, what are you onto exactly?" He sounded groggy.

"I've changed the hour to one-hundred and twenty minutes, to better suit my lifestyle."

"Good for you Boy, a noble venture! I'm proud of you! You've taken control of your own time."

"But that's not all, Plum. You'll be really proud of this, I've also shortened the minutes to thirty seconds, so that one-hundred and twenty minute hours don't seem very long at all!"

His left eye also opened, and I got the full Plum glare.

"Boy! What's the matter with you? One-hundred and twenty thirty-second-minute hours are what you began with. They're just blasted-confused sixty-second, sixty-minute hours."

I was a little hurt. "All right, Plum, if you're so smart, what would you do to time?"

"Well, you could try what I've been doing for years."

"What, Plum?"

"The nine day week!"

I did. It worked.

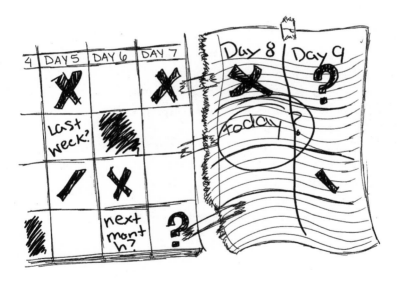

5. The Hole

I was walking through the woods behind my house, looking for Plum. I hadn't seen him in nearly a nine-day-week. This was strange. Since nine minutes rarely passed that we weren't together, nine days was very unusual. He was up to something.

Our woods were sort of thick, with plenty of evergreens, so once you got into them it was pretty dark. The pine needles made a soft padded blanket on the ground, so you could sneak around silently and surprise whoever it was that you decided to hunt down. Today I was hunting Plum.

The deeper I got, the darker it got, but I didn't mind. I knew the area well and the only predators there to worry about were us. The local squirrels and foxes kept out of range—we were deadeyes with a slingshot. And at eight years old we were much too scrawny for the local bears or mountain lions to bother with. No mammal there wanted anything to do with us. Plum was the only one I had to watch out for.

I was walking through the woods as quietly as possible, hoping that I would take Plum by surprise and have a laugh. In the end, of course, I got the surprise and Plum got the laugh.

I heard a strange sound nearby that sounded like someone digging through good old-fashioned Pennsylvania dirt with a pickaxe. But there was an echo. Then suddenly I was falling toward the center of the earth, downside-up, heels-over-head, spinning out of control. Luckily, I landed on my backside in an incredibly thick, pointy pile of pine bristles. I was unharmed—except for the indignity of having to pull hundreds of pine needles out of my butt. I looked around, and standing there next to me was a dirt-dark version of my friend Plum, with a substantial pickaxe at his side.

"Nice of you to drop in Boy," he said and laughed. "Do you need some help with those pine needles?"

"Thank you, Plum, no! I'm sure I'll manage!" I said, pulling a painfully long needle from my left buttock. "So this is where you've been for a week? Underground!" We were at least forty feet down a deep hole. And it wasn't a tight space either. Three or four people could have comfortably dined there around a table. Thrown over the hole's edge were rope ladders from some of the community's better tree houses, so that Plum could climb in and out of the hole easily. My friend had rigged up an ingenious system of levers, pulleys, and gadgets to move the loose earth from his hole up to the surface.

"Plum, what on Earth are you doing?"

"Under Earth."

"What?"

"Under Earth, what under Earth am I doing, you mean. I'm digging, that's what!"

He raised the pickaxe, and a large piece of dirt fell from the side of the hole.

"I can see that you're digging!" I was angry now. "But why are you digging Plum?"

"I'm looking for something, Boy!" He dumped several large shovelfuls of dirt and rock into a big box, then pulled on the lever beside him, which sent the box hurtling upward and out of the hole via rope and pulley. It returned four-fifths empty one-third of a minute later.

"It's not perfect, but it's good enough, eh Boy?"

It did work well—forty feet well in fact, with no signs of letting up. But what was he digging for?

"Is it treasure, or oil, or magic rocks you're looking for?"

He stopped digging and put down his tools.

"No Boy, though I have found some of those things. I'm digging for my middle name!"

He smiled his confident grin, certain that he was onto a good idea.

"You're digging for your what?"

"My middle name, Boy, my middle name. It's got to be down here somewhere!"

"Why on Earth . . ."

I stopped myself when I saw his eyes flash.

"Why under Earth (correcting myself) do you think your name is—under Earth?"

"Well it has to be somewhere, doesn't it, so why not underground?"

I guess he was right. Why not underground? And to be honest, I had forgotten that Plum had told me his middle name was missing, and I sure didn't want to hurt his feelings by telling him so. If it was important enough to dig a hole this deep to look for it, who was I to second-guess my best friend?

"OK brother, how can I help?"

"Start digging!"

He handed me a pick-axe.

So that's what we did, and we dug for days. It was satisfying work too, I have to admit. Though most people seem to be against digging—hard work, and all that—once you get a few feet down something changes and you develop a strange sense of accomplishment. There's nothing quite like looking up out of a deep hole you've dug for yourself. Try it. I'm sure you'll see what I mean. "Gravediggers are some of the happiest people on earth," Plum said. I could see why, though maybe you can't right now. Don't worry. Just set aside a weekend to dig, and you'll understand.

We dug, Plum and I, side by side, day after day. Each night we snuck home and hosed off before my parents saw us. Otherwise they might have figured out the nature of our latest mischief, and closed the hole thing down. It was going well.

"We're making great progress," Plum said.

Progress toward what I didn't *really* know, but it didn't matter. I was helping my friend, and it's the help that counts, and the friend, not what comes of it. Our hole was getting quite deep. After another nine-day-week had passed, we were seventy feet underground. By this time, we had mounted lights on our baseball batting helmets so we could see what we were doing. And down, down, down we went.

When you dig deep into the ground you find many odd things. I for instance found a ladies change purse filled with pennies and nickels, all dated 1907. They turned out to be really quite valuable. About fifty feet underground, Plum found a pillow. Under it was a bunch of teeth—children's teeth. We decided it was some Tooth Fairy plan gone wrong, so to avoid any bad Karma, we left the teeth buried in the wall for someone else to disturb.

We found a lot of spoons, if you want to know the truth. I don't know if it was because our hole was different from other people's holes, or because other diggers are also coming across lots of spoons, but this was our experience. Soup spoons and desert spoons, long spoons and short spoons, thin spoons and fat spoons, fancy spoons, silver spoons, brass spoons, serving spoons, and ladles. No forks.

"Aarrghh!" Plum screamed. "Where have you gone, middle name! I've seen enough spoons to last a lifetime!

I consoled him. Spoons can be boring.

"Plum, I don't mean to dig into your business, but why is it so important that we find your middle name, anyway?" I asked during one of our daily breaks. "We've been digging for weeks."

"You know Boy, I've been thinking about that myself. And I'm not sure I have the answer. But it just doesn't feel right to be wandering through life without a middle name. It makes me feel a little, well, incomplete. Empty inside. As far as I'm concerned, anyone who wants a middle name should have a middle name, and since I've lost mine, I intend to go on digging until I find it!"

I still had my middle name, so what did I know? You too probably. So I nodded my head and resumed digging. Just then I heard Plum's pickaxe come crashing down on something different than regular dirt. And it didn't make the classic clang-a-clang sound that spoons made either. It was solid. He moved in for a closer look, and started to brush away the loose pebbles clinging to what looked like a person's skull!

A shiver ran down my spine.

"What is that Plum? That's not a h-h-human sk-skull, is it?"

I was afraid. Murder or mayhem might be buried seventy feet below ground, in my backyard.

"It's a skull alright, but I'm not so sure it's human," Plum said.

He pulled the thing completely out of the dirt to inspect it more closely.

"Look how big this jaw is, and check out the forehead! It looks like Coach Klein, doesn't it?"

Coach Klein was our town's soccer guru, who had led the high school team to twenty-two state championships in a row. He also had a forehead that more than a few people thought was not human.

"No Boy, this is no human skull. It's Neanderthal!"

After unearthing the skull, Plum and I didn't dig so roughly in the hole. Before long, other bones began to turn up—legs, ribs, an arm. While Plum was digging out the skeleton, I continued to dig on the other side of our hole.

"Plum, look what I found. A left arm!"

I was excited to have completed the set.

"Boy, I don't mean to be rude, but I already found the left arm. It's leaning up against the wall over there."

"No Plum, I know a left arm when I see one, and this is a left arm or I'm a monkey!"

"Boy, you might be a monkey, or even a future internist, mortician, nurse, physical therapist, bone collector, or orthopedist for that matter. But I'm telling you that I already found the left arm, and here it is!"

Plum shoved the arm he had found in my face. So I did the same. So there we were, shoving left arms into each other's faces. Then we started to laugh. Since we'd both found left arms in the hole, we began looking for the matching right arms. My left arm was more delicate than Plum's. It was almost like they were from different species.

I continued working my side of the hole. Plum kept working on his thick Neanderthal skeleton. Soon I'd uncovered what I was sure would be a prized discovery—a completely intact hand.

"Plum, wait until you see this. I've got a hand that will blow your mind. It's completely intact."

"It can't be any more intact than the hand I just found. It's huge and perfect and—"

At that moment we banged heads. Plum and I were practically on top of each other. He had the hand he'd just found in his hand, and I had the hand I'd just found in mine, but those two hands were holding hands themselves! These two skeletons had gone to their graves together.

"What do you make of this, Plum?" I asked, because he seemed to know more about this than I did. After all, he knew that the skull we found first wasn't human.

"I don't know Boy. It's funny for sure. But these two hands definitely aren't from the same species."

When you looked at them right next to each other, you could see Plum was right. The small hand was like ours, with thin and fine fingers. The big hand was a crusher. Its thumb was massive and long—a little like Jack the Ape's thumb at the Pittsburgh zoo.

"What should we do now, Plum? Who should we tell?"

"I guess we should call the zoo."

I agreed, so we did. It turned out it wasn't the right group to call, of course, but what did we know? We were eight year olds. The zoo called someone else—a physical anthropologist, or an anthropological physicist, or something like that. Whatever he was, he knew an awful lot about dead people's bones, and he wasn't a half bad fellow, though he usually talked over our heads.

His name was Zeus Harrison, and this we liked a lot. It sounded like a Greek god. What he liked to be called, though, was Z, and from our perspective anyone named Z had to know what he was talking about. He was a savvy looking scientist—fairly young and really tall, with a square jaw and a long pony tail. He wore Hawaiian shirts and always had a group of students, colleagues, and reporters in tow. They, he insisted, had to walk behind Plum and me, because we were the 'discovery team,' and we should be paid our due. I think they held us in contempt but what did we care? It was our hole.

Z explained to us—and to the newspapers—that what we had found was awfully important. The big hand was definitely hominoid, or mankind-like, from "the tertiary period of the Cenozoic era, right at the end of the Paleocene epoch." But this big male Neanderthal was holding the hand of a female Homo sapiens—"and if Leakey or Johanson disagreed, they could kiss my butt!" Z had a way with words.

Z talked about this phalanx and that joint derivative and how this cultural stage overlapped with that cultural stage. Very scientific, but as far as Plum and I could tell, what we had discovered was that Homo sapiens and Neanderthals didn't fight and kill each other, until the big guys went extinct. No, they dated! Z likened this relationship to a 1960s love-in—something he was very familiar with, but we had to *google* it.

So a new theory developed about the origins of mankind, and Plum and I got quite a lot of credit. Neanderthals and Homo sapiens weren't quite as bloodthirsty as previously thought, and almost everyone was happy to know that. Z's analysis also made it a lot easier for the world to accept inter-racial relationships. Heck, if two subspecies were getting it on 200,000 years ago, why was everyone so uptight now? So our hole brought about a rebirth of the free love revolution, and the world was much better off for it.

In his scientific paper, Z gave me credit for the find, and at my recommendation he named the skeleton, "Plumepithecus larensis, the Neanderthal boyfriend!"

I teased Plum about this a lot, but he took it in stride. Unfortunately, all of the anthropological hubbub meant we had to turn the hole over to the National Academy of Physical Anthropology. That was OK, but I was sad that we couldn't spend any more time down there, hanging out and digging up spoons.

"Plum, I'm sorry we didn't find your middle name," I said to my best friend. "Maybe it will turn up someplace else."

"Don't worry old pal," he replied. "Plumepithicus was worth it. And besides, there's plenty more holes we can dig ourselves into."

Which we surely did.

6. Hail to the Sleet

We were nine years old—on the brink of completing our first decade. The gods were smiling down on us, unloading mountains of snow on Seasoncreek before Christmas break. When there wasn't any sign of the snow letting up by December 21st, Mr. Pringle, a great superintendent who years later would be forced into retirement after being caught embezzling two hundred dollars from our Statue of Liberty fund, declared the district closed until well after the New Year. Life was great.

Plum and I constructed a maze of elaborate tunnels in the snow between our houses so that we didn't have to show our faces to the adult world for hours or even days on end. Our snow cave was stocked with enough provisions to sustain us through at least four missed meals. Sleeping bags, tunnels packed with straw, and an ingenious lighting system rigged up by Plum that used the sun, two flashlights and sixteen mirrors, provided us with every comfort we could ask for in our under-snow world. The other kids in the neighborhood made several attempts to invade our fortress, but Plum and I kept watch from a battle station in the fort, and with the substantial ammunition we kept in reserve, we held them off. We also let Moses, our dog, roam freely in the yard (atop mountains of snow), so that most of our playmates wouldn't take even two steps onto the property. Unless Moses was sniffing out some fool squirrel who had forgotten to hibernate, our territory seemed secure.

"Boy, I've been thinking about our future business life together. You know money may come in handy when we're old."

"You mean when we're in our twenties, Plum?"

"Or thirties, even. Older anyway. Someday we'll want things, although I can't imagine what, and we'll need money to buy 'em."

"Do you mean we'll have to pay for things with our own money?"

"Who did you think would pay?"

"I don't know. Our parents, I guess."

"No, Boy. They'll die, or retire, or both, and then we start paying."

"I suppose you're right, Plum. What business do you think will be good? Investment? Law? Banking?" I asked, naming possibly the three most avaricious occupations known to man.

"None of those. We're going to be gamblers, Boy. Bookies. Only we're not going to play around with twenty-year-old multi-billionaire athletes who fix games, shave points, or lay down for a payday. I have a plan to eliminate the human element from gambling. We're going to make gambling totally unpredictable, so that it exists in its purest form. Like art!" Plum's voice reached a crescendo as the idea boiled his blood.

"You see Boy, gambling is life, and life is a gamble. But we are after the pure outcome. No sports scandals for us."

I marveled at Plum's passion for a pure and unpredictable game to the last. "May the best man win" was important to him, but here he was, calculating a way to remove the man from the win.

"It's not possible, Plum. People will always mess up a perfect game."

"You're suggesting then that every baseball diamond has its flaw, even if it's too small for the trained eye to see. Not true, Boy, although until recently I might have agreed with you. We're going to take gambling to a new level. To the sky! To the heavens!"

I liked the plan to be gamblers. It sounded fun. But I was beginning to wonder if Plum was on some kind of mind-altering substance. Gambling as a spiritual exercise seemed ridiculous.

"Come on, Plum. The heavens? Did someone spike your juice this morning?"

"You're missing the point, Boy. We're actually going to bet on the heavens. We're going to be the first Weather Gamblers. And once we have the rights to the sky, everyone who wants a piece of the action is going to have to come through us!"

I just shook my head, and got up to take my turn at the watch.

"Did you know that gambling has been around almost forever?" Plum said, stopping me.

"I wasn't aware of that."

"It's true. The Neanderthals are known to have been big fans of a game very similar to craps."

"Are you crazy, Plum? They didn't have dice."

"I know that, Boy! Bones! They used the finger bones of sheep!"

I didn't even know sheep had fingers.

"If you don't believe me, just ask Z!" Plum was reading my mind. "The Egyptians were card players five thousand years ago. Where do you think the game 'Pharaoh' comes from?"

He had a point.

"And hunter-gatherers were laying odds on mammoth kills and cheetah races from day one! Gambling's been with us forever, Boy. It's part of the collective unconscious. But not *weather* gambling, amigo. This one is ours!"

After a while it began to sink in. No one could fix the weather, but we could set the odds with some confidence. You'd really have to pay for the short money, if you wanted to bet on snow in Alaska. Same with betting on sunshine— but rain paid fifty to one in January. The temperature over/ under in Cairo on July 4th was 109 degrees Fahrenheit. The line for overcast days in Seattle in April is twenty-seven. You could bet on June's snowfall in Nova Scotia, or annual rainfall in Brazil, but if you wanted a real long shot, there was hail in Timbuktu at 500,000 to 1. There wasn't any meteorological element we couldn't place odds on, and as long as we lay off the bets ourselves, Plum and I would take our 10% to the bank. Heck, we'd lay odds on a meteor shower if suckers wanted that action.

Plum was right, it was pure and perfect. Everyone talked about the weather anyway, so why not bet on it? For us, the business was like winning the daily lottery without buying a ticket. And the event played every day, for free, all across the globe.

The Idea Man

Years later, when we had grown into the immature and unjaded adults we had always hoped to become, Plum violated our rule (we weren't to place bets ourselves) and made us a small fortune when he miraculously predicted a foot of sleet on a June day in Barcelona. He'd studied historic sleet patterns over the European continent for months, and he even convinced me to contribute a few dollars to his wager—against my better judgment. The research paid off. Plum had discovered that every five hundred and thirty-six years a fierce weather front created by the Balthanese Mountains causes sleet to fly over Spain. But only on June 14th.

We waited sixteen years for the right day to arrive, and then wagered one hundred dollars—fifty each. Courtesy of 270,000 to 1 odds, we made millions! That money would pay for the musings and wanderings of our middle, late middle, early old, middle old, late old, and old, old age. No two people on Earth appreciated icy rain more than us after that miserable-wonderful Spanish day.

7. Brother

"A younger brother is an excellent thing to have," Plum said, "he's bound to make you seem responsible."

Mine arrived when I was six years, seven months, and three days old. At six, one doesn't expect a sibling. They just show up and you adjust. Since my brother was fairly loud and very smelly, I adjusted by spending more time with Plum. But once the bad smells wore off, and he quieted down, I grew to like Brother Ben quite a lot.

He was an elf-child, with a shag of white hair, bright blue eyes, and an impish grin that always hinted at some horrible mischief. There was also a measure of genius in him, making him much more treacherous—endearing, but treacherous. When we were older, our neighbors caused him a lot of trouble. Every time Brother hit a ball into their yard they yelled at him, called our parents, and kept the ball. Each time they called he got grounded. Over two summers, Brother lost fifteen balls to that ogre clan bordering our property. Now he wanted his balls back, and some revenge.

These neighbors had a horrible beast of a canine, Brutus by name, patrolling their property. He seemed one part bear and one part mountain lion, but in truth, he was just 100% large brown dog. We called him The Brute. That dog disliked everyone, with a single exception. Over the years, Brother had secretly fed the beast through the fence separating our yards, so now he was putty in Brother's little hands. Plum and I had benefited from this strange bond on our runs through the town sprinklers. Every other dog in the county had attacked us. Brother's secret pet did not.

That summer, when our nasty neighbor went off to work as a corporate raider or futures trader or pork belly specialist, Brother began work of his own: training the beast. Each morning, after the neighbor's flashy red sports car had rolled out of the garage, Brother crept into their yard with scraps of meat from our dinner the night before. I didn't pay too much attention at first, but Plum took an early interest in Brother's rituals. Sometimes Brother would take a spool of bright red ribbon with him. Other times he took a can of red spray paint. We'd watch him, Plum and me, but all we would see was my little brother, three-feet-tall with a white bush of hair, dashing across the yard, The Brute in tow.

The summer wore on and so did this routine. Then one morning, I noticed Brother was still in bed, long after his usual wake-up hour. So I climbed up into his bunk and jumped on him a bit, as older brothers are free to do.

"Why are you still in bed? What about The Brute? Don't you have something to do with him?" I said, pinning the imp-elf on his back.

"Boy," he yelled, "get off of me! It's done. Leave me alone. I'm sleeping in today!"

"Not until you tell me what you've been up to! I've been watching you and that animal all summer. I want to know now, and you're not going anywhere until you tell me!"

He clammed up. No matter what I tried, that brother of mine wouldn't tell me what he'd been doing with the dog-monster. I pounded him for a while—something else older brothers are also free to do—then I tickled him before finally resorting to blackmail. I failed completely. Brother had a will of iron. Someday, he would become a first class spy. All he would tell me was that his revenge for all of the lost baseballs and soccer balls and volleyballs and tennis balls was imminent, and that if I kept my eyes open I might see it in action. So I waited.

Plum and I camped out in the tree fort we had built the year before as a lookout for strange events. It had a panoramic view of our bad neighbor's yard. We took shifts watching, but at first nothing was different. Soon however we started to notice some strange changes in the town's behavior.

Guest and Johnson's Born Again Carpet Cleaning Company—don't get me started on evangelical carpet cleaners—began making daily calls to Wallace's house. Sometimes three or four times a day. Within a week, they were ripping up Wallace's red rugs, and trashing them in a huge disposal bin. Curious household possessions also began showing up on the curb—a sweat suit, a pair of Wallace's really expensive cowboy boots, then books, including Webster's Dictionary, and nearly every volume of the Harvard classics.

Brother strutted past Wallace's garbage pile every morning with a smile on his face, but he still wouldn't tell me what was happening. Finally, though, the pieces of the puzzle came together.

It was early on Saturday morning that I saw Wallace putting The Brute out to pee. The dog raced over to the brand new convertible Wallace had just bought—fancy jet

The Idea Man

black on the outside, with a devil-red leather interior that matched the man. The dog leapt up onto the hood of the car and peed right into it, all over its innards, then it trotted over to our street's fire hydrant and peed there too, before finally urinating on the new red trim of Wallace's house. Wallace stood open-mouthed, watching this spectacle.

'Incredible," I thought. "Brother trained The Brute to pee on all of Wallace's red stuff.

"Incredible indeed," Plum said, "because dogs are supposed to be color-blind! But things are never black or white, and especially when they're red!"

In the following weeks, the flood of clothing, furniture, and carpet slowed to a trickle. And Wallace pulled into his garage in a shiny new *blue* convertible.

8. Good Monk, Bad Monk

When we were eleven, Plum took a keen interest in religion. Until then, he had been indifferent to the "God Show," as he called it. Now nothing else seemed to matter to him, and nothing else would do for our entertainment.

There were several religious denominations in Seasoncreek. The Presbyterians had always been the best-dressed Christians in town. They were all business. In fact, more business deals went down at their 10:00 am service than could be counted—and they had lots of accountants in their midst. We Jews were a much smaller deal in Seasoncreek. Since only four Jewish families lived there, and the one from Ethiopia spoke only Amharech, we kept our religion to ourselves.

It was the Catholics that Plum found the most interesting. From time out of mind, Seasoncreek had a monastery in its precious hills, tucked snugly-smugly between the estates that dominated The Heights, as the area was known to the blue bloods who lived there.

This was considered one of the fabulous places on earth to live, with no estate amounting to less than five hectares. Each family had a clear lineage running back

The Idea Man

to some robber baron or another—gas, oil, or banking money from the time of the industrial revolution up to the present. Yes, there was a lot of money in The Heights, but very little trickle down.

"Money, unlike water, runs upstream," Plum said.

So the people of Seasoncreek were familiar with the joys and splendor of both splendor (meaning money) and asceticism, thanks to The Heights. A monastery among fields of gold! Monks and corporate heads living together, but dining separately!

Many days after school, Plum and I would hike The Heights to explore the mysteries of the monastic order. Sometime in the 18th century, a man named Alyosius Yablonski had constructed a colossal house that later became Seasoncreek's monastery. A wooden palace surrounded by a dense oak forest, this building had the most incredible doors anyone could imagine. Though few of the Seasoncreek monks were ever celebrated for their piety, they were famous far and wide for their woodworking, and for nearly three centuries they furnished the world's elite with entranceways suitable for kings. Yablonski trained the first monks in master carpentry before he met his own Maker, and the tradition continued forever after. As boys, though, we were less interested in the spectacular doors, and more interested in what went on behind them.

For many months we prowled the monastery's grounds, observing all of the Brothers' activities and rituals. All were master carpenters—in the tradition of Jesus Christ himself, I suppose, although I've heard that he was a relatively poor roofer and one of the reasons he ultimately became a prominent prophet instead. But an interest in carpentry was where the Monks' similarities to Jesus ended.

Most of the Seasoncreek holy kept at their work, carving out religious history without equal from dawn until dark, and beyond. Since almost every waking moment was devoted to the craft, the religious activities occurred right before sunrise, or extremely late at night. Lumbermen kept finely cut oak pouring into the monastery's gates; no idle hand ever had time to shed a callous. The elite from around the wide world came to collect the magical doors that had been chopped, carved, and finished within the inner sanctums. The woodwork was so well known—legendary in fact—that the world paid handsomely for even the smallest shutter. And the monastery became rich—rich beyond belief. And where money gathers, troubles follow.

In our observations, two monks stood out in our minds. Plum named them Good Monk and Bad Monk. Good Monk was a kindly, god-fearing man who loved to feed the squirrels. They would take nuts from his hand. Bad monk kicked the monastery dog. Good Monk read stories out loud, and pretended not to see us when we spied on him. He whistled Mozart and smiled at the sunshine even as it beat down on him in his brown wool robes. Bad Monk cursed the sunshine, hollered at us to get off of his land, and never whistled. He spat a lot.

Bad Monk labored through his lot in life, counting money all day long. He ordered the other Brothers to work until their hands bled like the stigmata. He hated women, nuns in particular, but especially buyers, muttering under his breath whenever any of them passed through the monastery's gates. Good Monk seemed thankful for every day. He also had a girlfriend. Even if they come from the same stock, it's amazing how different people can be. When I took this up with Plum, he would only comment, "No two monks are alike."

The Idea Man

Good Monk's girlfriend was a beautiful young sprite, not much more than eighteen years old. He must have been forty. She had flowery golden curls and a giddy laugh, sweet to the taste. Plum and I liked her as we watched from high in the Great Oak just outside the monastery's walls. She glided through the forest, eluding branches and bramble like a dryad, until she came to the hidden gate that opened into Good Monk's courtyard. A secret knock, and she was through.

Good Monk greeted her with a kiss. She would sit down beside him, or pick flowers for her hair from the rose briar growing up the walls, or just doze in the sun. He looked at her as he worked—she was the angel in his carving.

From our outpost, Plum and I could see both Good Monk and Bad Monk at the same time. It was all the same air, not one molecule different, but they breathed so differently— Good Monk with ease, and Bad Monk like each breath would be his last. Watch people breathing, and you'll see how much trouble some of them have. "Breathing is an important part of life, and it's not automatic," Plum said up in that tree.

Then one day, when an afternoon was wearing on, we watched the lives of Good and Bad Monk change forever. Bad Monk was in his usual foul mood. He had stomped on the holy dog's tail four times in an hour, so we knew that trouble was brewing. Good Monk was at work on a fast-growing masterpiece, more incredible than anything he had ever attempted before. It was a trellis, one that depicted his angel in an embrace with all the wonders of the forest—bees, bears and bramble, holly, streams and wildflowers. It was perfect enough to make you smile. No tears or awe—a smile.

"God touched that one," Plum said, "if He exists."

At that moment, Bad Monk came storming into Good Monk's courtyard, catching him and his lovely girl completely by surprise. She was asleep, covered only by her golden locks and the thinnest sundress on this good earth, while Good Monk bent over his work playing out the final delicate strokes of his art.

We couldn't hear what Bad Monk said, but given the look on his face, it must have been awful. Then he grabbed Good Monk's girlfriend by her hair and lifted her up. She let out a cry and in a flash Good Monk was on him, removing her from Bad Monk's terrible hands. The Good Monk gently led her to the secret door, kissed her hand and sent her off to safety. This only took a few seconds, but that was more than enough time for Bad Monk to pick up an axe, and wreck some havoc.

The Idea Man

My eyes must have been pretty wide when I turned to Plum.

"That's how it is with creation, Boy," he said. "A year in the making, a second in the breaking."

By the time Good Monk could get between the demon and his damage, Bad Monk had completely destroyed the trellis. Since the entire incident had been quite loud, the whole monkish populace soon had assembled at Good Monk's doorway. By then, Good Monk and Bad Monk were in the throes of an exchange so heated that even we could make out certain words. Bad Monk was screaming, "devotion, restraint, and subservience."

Good Monk chanted, "love, passion, contemplation and bliss" right back at him.

The words and spittle continued to fly as the rest of the community slipped into the courtyard, circling Good Monk and Bad Monk within a human monk-ring. It looked like a cockfight with two monks instead of roosters, set within a monastery in Seasoncreek Heights, decorated with wooden paneling meant for the Gods, instead of in some field, or in a seedy alley littered with garbage.

Good Monk and Bad Monk eventually crossed each other's emotional line. "You keep that Siren out of my holy place of work!" Bad Monk screeched.

"She's an Angel not a Siren," Good Monk replied, "and I wouldn't call what you do work. You're a whittler!"

The monks in audience let out a gasp. *Whittler* was the worst slur possible to them—a curse if there ever was one. Bad Monk picked up an unfinished chair leg, partially decorated with devils, demons, and hell fire, and swung it at Good Monk's head. Good Monk grabbed a three-foot tall crucifix with the visage of the Holy Father carved on it to fend off Bad Monk's attack.

At the outset, the monks were wagering on who would win the fight. Money changed hands, as Good and Bad Monk traded heavy blows with their respective symbols. Half were loyal to Good Monk, the other half to the Bad. Good versus evil in the heart of Seasoncreek! But soon betting on the battle wasn't enough. Grudges and vendettas surfaced, and all the Monks waded into the fray—a real, honest-to-goodness holy war.

Now hand-to-hand monk combat had turned into a battlefield. Bad monks biting good monks, good monks eye-gouging bad monks. Everyone bashing everyone else with whatever woodwork they could get their hands on. Finally, Plum and I scrambled down our oak and called the Heights' swollen-ruddy-faced-bug-eyed police chief.

When the police got there to sort out the carnage, we had moved in for a closer look. No one was too badly hurt, but five years worth of irreplaceable woodcarving had been reduced to splinters. Some monks were taken to the local emergency room for treatment of scrapes, splinters, and small lacerations. Others were sent to their rooms. Bad Monk spat on the chief's shoe when he decided that the chief was taking Good Monk's side. The result was a trip downtown and a night in the pokey to cool off.

The police wrote up the monastery for disturbing the peace, and fined them heavily.

"Anyone will fight over pride Boy," Plum said as we walked down from the Heights, "especially if they think that they're holier than you."

As for me, that monk brawl left a lasting impression. Most people in Seasoncreek condemned the wood-carving monks for having a street fight over a girl. I however, developed a new respect for the passions of the men of God.

9. The Plum System

Immortality is hard to come by, but some people stumble backwards into it, and of course Plum did.

"It's human nature to want to be remembered," he said, "even if it's for something stupid."

A man will juggle balls for three days if it will get his name into some record book or another. Somebody else will eat one hundred and six hard-boiled eggs in an hour. But great individuals have a natural way of making history, without using balls or eating eggs.

I was always certain that Plum was going to be great—I just wasn't sure how or why. Would an idea of his spark the imaginations of the people around him? Or would he step up to the plate during an international crisis? Something big was bound to happen. But curiously, long before Plum did become great, a man named Wolfgang Bug, a man of discovery, declared that Plum's immortality was assured.

There's discovery everywhere when you're twelve years old—up in trees and down every hole, behind abandoned buildings, and especially across the railroad tracks. But twelve isn't really a time for self-exploration—not consciously anyhow. Most twelve-year-olds don't spend much time on introspection, which is why we were so free to seek out curious adventures then. Plum believed that our greatest discoveries would come in the most obvious, and therefore the least expected, places. I looked hard for magic in the world. He sat back, and laughed at my struggles.

"Don't think so hard, Boy," he said. "It can only hurt the team. That's the first trick to figuring out anything really important. Whatever you want to discover is probably right in front of your face."

"In front of my face, Plum?"

"Yeah or in front of mine," he said, raising his eyebrows.

Professor Bug was a very stout astronomer—five feet tall and three feet thick, with receding hair and nearly inch-thick spectacles. His sideburns dated him by at least twenty years. Bug lived a hermit's life in a one-room loft just beneath our town's observatory. Every night the professor scanned the ebony sky for new stars and active systems. A lonely man's job, except he wasn't alone very often, because Plum and I searched the sky with him.

It was our habit to sneak out of bed at two a.m. and join Bug for hours of travel through time and space. He especially encouraged us in the summer, when school was replaced by pastimes like baseball or swimming—neither his specialty. In truth, we had only a brief window of interest in space as children, that summer when we were twelve, and willing to sit still for hours beneath a giant telescope. We didn't care about girls enough yet, I suppose, but for a while, Plum and I trekked out to Wolfgang's telescope every night to learn about heaven.

By the 4th of July, we knew all the common constellations, the two Dippers (Big and Little), Cassiopeia, Orion, the Snowy Run, Ooshius, Erac and all the others. We could tell planets from stars, supernovas from vacuous anomalies, and deep space from near—well, you get the idea. With all the important stars and formations firmly set in the back pockets of our young minds, we might have begun to find Professor Wolfgang Bug and his telescope boring. But that was exactly the moment when things heated up for us in Bug's observatory.

He trusted us completely with the movements of his fantastic telescope. Under his tutelage we had become as proficient at scanning the sky as any of his long-gone, brainiac graduate students—or so he said. We were just shorter, so we needed a boost to get to the eyepiece. Two cushions and a copy of Copernicus' *Principi de Celestii* did the trick. Swinging that scope 360 degrees was like riding a rollercoaster in a thunderstorm. Light crashed down on the mind from new angles at every second. One of us would fly the heavenly skies, while the other napped at Bug's feet, dreaming of light traveling from time out of mind. And he sat back, waiting for our young eyes to spark his middle-aged mind. That's how it worked.

You see, Bug had been stargazing forever. After starting at four years old, he had his doctorate from some institute in Stockholm by seventeen. This prodigy was a stellar freak at thirty. Bug was so hot that no one could work with him—no one, that is, but two twelve year old boys on the brink of either a great discovery or puberty. (I wonder now whether they were the same thing.)

Bug had seen the sky from almost every angle during his lifetime. But so many observations, so many trips through the Universe alone, had rendered him blind through habit. He needed new eyes, new visions. Ours. So while we swung through the lights, describing what we saw, or thought we saw, he sat with his eyes closed, filling in the starry gaps of our observations. Night after night that summer, the clouds dispersed, the rains stayed away, and we three wandered on high.

In late August, just three weeks before we would start at the junior high school, something happened while I was exploring the near reaches of our Universe. Plum was running around the observatory while I called out the names of one star formation after another. He told me what he remembered about its neighbors, and Bug told me where to look next. I was in a bad mood, because Wolfgang B. had me circling back to one patch of sky over and over again. As twelve-year-olds always do, I was getting mad, bored and restless.

"I know what's here, Bug. You know what's here. Even your graduate students know what's here!" I said. "Can't we move on please?"

He didn't answer—just kept directing me back to where I had just been. Perhaps at some time long past, Bug had imagined there was a shadow in this part of the sky, and now he wanted youthful eyes to re-re-re-examine it.

Plum taunted me with the names of the same stars again, just to piss me off. This combination of Bug making me repeat myself, and Plum mocking me when I did, finally did it. I let the scope stand still, and when Plum ran by me the next time I tripped him, sending him flying headlong across the room into Bug's marble desk. A long and wide gash opened on my best friend's forehead. He let out a yelp, and I ran over to assess the damage. I felt badly, but not so badly that I was going to relinquish my evening at the telescope, or apologize to him. Plum got what he deserved.

But before I got to him, Plum was carefully, scientifically, examining the slash on his head.

"Boy," he said. "Are you aware that I have a quasi-nebular constellation of moles on my brow?"

"What do you think, Professor," I asked with a laugh. Bug picked up a small mirror from a nearby table, and held it over Plum's bloody forehead.

"Do you see what I feel, Professor?" Plum asked our mentor.

"I do!" Bug said. "It looks like the fleeting tail of Ooshius. Yes! That's it! This is what I've been looking for! Take us there, Boy!"

So I did. I took us twenty parsecs and five at one hundred and eight degrees from Ooshius, and there it was. An undiscovered system!

I was shocked. We were shocked. The world was shocked the next day. And we danced around the observatory, blood dripping from one brow, sweat from another. (Bug was rather out of shape). This new system — the Plum System, I named it—was closer to us than anyone could have conceived. Our great grandchildren will probably travel to it in a very modest spaceship. I inspected more closely the place on Plum's forehead where a curious line of moles had been magically connected with a distant freckle by a gash, and the heavens had been revealed.

"You see what I mean, Boy?" Plum said, raising his now-bloody eyebrows again. "Discovery takes place in the strangest places. Right in front of your face! Or even, right in your friend's face!"

So the Plum System was discovered in the now famous Wolfgang Bug Observatory, first on the forehead of my closest friend, and then in the heavens. So Larry Plum became immortal.

10. Monster

The sightings in the Northern Territory came so suddenly and frequently that even the experts were speechless. It had been more than ten years since anyone had seen the creature in North America, and even then, no one had any real evidence.

This time was different. Here we were, an advanced 21st-century civilization, with computers, fighter jets, laser guided smart bombs, and individually packaged single-serving ketchup, all stirred up over the monster known as Bigfoot.

For Plum and I, the incredible thing was that we didn't encounter the monster only in the newspapers. We were fourteen when we were sent off to summer camp, and it was there that we came to know Big Foot.

It can be a bit scary going off to camp for the first time, and especially when your parents are sending you to a rugged Survivor Man type place like the one our parents had chosen for us. They wanted to instill a love for nature in us, I guess, but we felt condemned to a summer of discipline away from our usual haunts, the home of our minds' idle wandering. This experience was also supposed to be "good for us," so basically it promised to feel bad.

Canada is big country, and Plum and I were sent way up into it, where mass transit fears to tread. Since North Camp was a thousand miles north of Seasoncreek, by August 15th fall was not only falling, but fallen, and an early winter seemed to be at hand. None of North Camp had ever been logged, and only sections of it explored. Its caretakers claimed that it would be the last uncut swath of real estate in North America. The trees were tall, and the wildlife dense and copious.

After eight weeks at North Camp, Plum and I had gotten tired of the wilds and each other. To nurture our independence, our vigilant guides had weaned themselves from us, as they're expected to do. We had become comfortable with very long hikes alone in the wilderness, and Plum was spending lots of time completely off by himself. I suspect he was looking around for what he truly believed he had lost. His middle name.

I was less inclined to range widely on my own. There were too many bears near North Camp. Still, Plum and I had a routine that seemed OK to us—best friends, but a little more independent.

I was gutting a fish for breakfast at dawn when our oldest camp guide, Pete, came tearing past me screaming, "Monster, monster, monster!"

I tried to ask him what had happened, but he flew by me, stepping hard on my left foot as he passed. Two days later old Pete was found in an exhausted heap, thirty miles down river near a small town called Happenstance. He babbled for two hours about a hairy eight-foot tall monster with twenty-four-inch feet (two-foot feet doesn't sound scary somehow). Then Pete got carted South, to a distant psychiatric hospital.

A few minutes after Pete went by, Plum arrived, and asked why I had my left shoe off. I told him about Pete stomping me hard on his way by, and how I was having a look for trauma. Since neither of us had any idea what might have spooked our guide, we went on with our usual business. A couple of days passed before news began to trickle into our small camp that might account for old running Pete.

It seems there had been a few odd sightings in our neck of the North woods. Old Ham Wood, a spry eighty-eight year old logger, saw a giant bear sitting cross-legged on a stump, reading a weathered copy of the Upanishads. Maggie Fox, the general storekeeper in Jackson, swore she saw something similar guzzling down a cafe latte on one of her daily nature walks. Ninety-nine year old Rory Buck, the camp cook, tripped in what he described as an eight-inch deep footprint while running a huge bear out of his wild mushroom stock. And then there was Pete—running thirty miles away from some Canadian Chewbacca. Something big was clearly afoot. But was it Bigfoot?

Lacking dinosaurs, and any credible evidence of extra-terrestrial life in our galaxy (the landing at Rockwood Four occurred about ten years later), our generation relied on myths like the Lock Ness monster and stories about Area 51 to feed our imaginations. The Bigfoot sightings started near North Camp turned the world's head in our direction. But would its ears listen to the ramblings of geriatrics?

At first, the verdict was hallucinations. Ham Wood, Mag Fox, and Old Rory Buck had logged two hundred and seventy-six years between them. But new sightings soon followed that couldn't be so easily ignored.

One afternoon, Plum and I were on a mission to collect rare berries. We hadn't had any luck near base camp, so we threw on our daypacks and set off into the Westwoods, some distance from North Camp. About five miles out, our fortunes changed. It rained fluxomberries, dogberries, and tastiest of all, blue-green-redberries. One patch led to another, and before we knew it, we had collected thirty pounds of pie filling—each. But it was also getting dark, and neither of us thought we could make it back to North Camp without some light. This wasn't a big problem. We were camping alone every night—just not in the Westwoods. Neither of us knew the area, and our camp guides always stressed knowing your terrain, so they were certain to be irritated by what they would undoubtedly call a "berry misadventure."

Still, we had to make the most of our oversight. We laid out our packs in the rooty-crook of a giant sycamore. We snacked on the wildberries, absorbed the sounds of the wild, and retold each other stories of our past. I then slipped off into forest dreamland, only to be aroused by an extraordinary aroma.

"Plum, do you smell that? That's mushrooms frying in butter, or I'm a wood elf!"

He didn't answer, and it was so dark on that moonless night that I couldn't even see if he was there. But in the near distance—maybe 100 yards off—a small fire was casting light in a clearing.

I was now sure that Plum wasn't around. No one could have ignored that smell. No, Plum had clearly headed for that campfire and its pungent feast—and I was alone in the dark woods.

The Idea Man

This wouldn't do. A mysterious campfire, and a mushroom banquet nearby, with Plum already on the trail? I followed my nose, and made for the fire and my friend. With each step, the mushrooms became more and more tantalizing—not pungent, but magical. When my nostrils flared, it was like an appetizer, and each deep breath was a main course.

Three camp fires were burning, coals glowing red-mercury on the ground. On a griddle over each fire, an obsidian pot simmered the natural juices that the forest provided.

What shook me, though, was who was presiding over this country kitchen. Plum was there, his gangly fourteen-year-old body draped in a cooking smock, with a large stirring spoon in his left hand. Next to him stood a monster, no less than eight feet and four inches tall, with thick curly mahogany hair covering his body. It was thickest over his face, where a massive forked and double braided beard could easily house three squirrels and a family of sparrows. The creature nodded his approval as Plum stirred one of the massive black kettles. I was edging back behind a tree when the creature spoke.

"Come!" the man-monster boomed, waving me toward him with his giant hand, now totally concealed by an oven mitt. "Come and join us! Have some supper!"

Plum smiled at me, stabbing his grin right into my belly. Then he turned to his companion.

"Sir, this is Boy, my best friend. Boy, meet Walter Bigfoot."

"Call me Walt, all my friends do. And pull up a stump and a bowl. Soup's just about ready."

Walt? I was completely tongue tied, so I did just that, sitting down to midnight supper with Larry Plum and Walter Bigfoot, the nicest monster you'd ever want to meet. Bigfoot told Plum about the base of his mushroom soup, what thickener he preferred, and why you couldn't let mushrooms a la Rousse come to a full boil. Apparently they lost their wild essence over 180 degrees Fahrenheit. And me? This was all too much to take.

The Idea Man

Much to my relief, Walt turned out to be a vegetarian chef. He specialized in wild mushroom dishes, which was why he was always spotted in odd and far away places, following the fungi as they came into season across North America. His wife lived in Saskatchewan. I didn't ask.

As I ate my soup that night, out of a bowl carved from a maple burl, each sip expanded and bent my mind. His was a psychedelic culinary tour de force, a bouillabaisse base for the meninges. We were shroomed! As sleep overtook me and my illusions became dreams, Plum and Bigfoot discussed the meaning of life and the secret of good broth. When Plum and I woke up later than usual the next day, Mr. Bigfoot and his natural kitchen had vanished. Only a trail of extremely large footprints leading North remained. Walter Bigfoot was gone.

As for me, though my brain and palate cried out for more of Walt's cooking, my body had clearly had its fill. The colors of the sunrise were waaaaayyyy out of kilter. The oaks were laughing at themselves for becoming so tall. On our way back to base camp, a fox stopped to ask me for directions, and . . . well, let's leave it at that.

When we got back to North Camp late that afternoon, every authority figure from one hundred miles around was waiting for us. My parents had called the night before, hoping to talk to their "baby." Since neither Plum nor I could be found, my mother had a fit—not epileptic, but close. Search parties had headed out in every direction, but they couldn't track us in the dark.

To make things even more exciting, the next morning there was another monster sighting—this time by a park ranger fishing on the edge of the Westwoods. He called headquarters and mobilized still another group of local trackers—lunatics with hound dogs, for the most part.

Almost before they could set out, though, there were six more sightings of a lumbering hairy goliath who matched exactly what Old Ham, Maggie, and Rory had described. That night, one amateur photograph of Walt appeared on the national news, and all hell broke loose. Every big game hunter from all four corners of this round Earth was soon on a jet plane, headed for the Northern Territory.

The North Camp population rose from sixteen to sixteen hundred in forty-eight hours. The ancient woods were awash in neon-orange hunting parkas. There were so many semi-automatic hunting rifles that ordinarily I would have been afraid for the deer population! But it was Walt they were after, as our summer natural nursery suddenly became a killers' circus.

A cadre of slender, pointy-nosed men in black suits and sunglasses dragged us into a run-down cabin, and interrogated us about our night in the woods. What had we seen? Hear any strange noises? What did we smell? Had we been accosted by any eight-foot tall monsters meeting the traditional description of Bigfoot? I'm not sure why Plum and I didn't tell them anything but I suspect it was instinct. They were killers on the loose.

Unfortunately, it wasn't long before the agents found our footprints mixed in with Walt's, and the questions got more pointed. But I didn't trust these people, and especially since Walt had been so pleasant. So what if he was big and hairy? Sometime in life everyone has at least one friend with too much back hair. I figured he could use a head start for his escape, and I was going to give it to him.

They continued to bully us, until I figured Walt was safe. Then I reacted to their rudeness by breaking my silence.

"Soup!" I yelled.

"What, son? What did you say?"

"Bigfoot cooked us mushroom soup, and went on his way. He's smart and cultured and he knows the woods. You'll never catch him!"

"Oh, we'll find him, son. We find all the monsters!" And they left.

Then Plum turned to me.

"Who's more monstrous, Boy? The hunters or the hunted?"

Days passed without a shot. Except for Walt's footprints, no other part of him turned up.

In our final weeks at North Camp, before returning to Seasoncreek and our first term in high school, we kept an eye out for Walt. We went back to the Westwoods, and had dinner together, but no Bigfoot. We talked with Old Rory, Ham, and Maggie, but no other adults wanted to believe that we had made soup with a monster. Our experiences at North Camp would recede into the annals of modern myth, just as the men in black receded back under the stones that they had crawled out from in the first place. A big mystery, with no blood spilled. Near the end of our time there, we even began to doubt ourselves a bit.

So as we packed up our sacks on our last night at North Camp, Plum and I felt that our unconfirmed Westwoods dream was gone for good, giving way to the adult world waiting for us 1000 miles south. But the next morning, after we boarded the train back to Seasoncreek, I dug into my pack for a deck of cards to occupy us, and found a coarse envelope made from the bark of a paper birch tree.

"Plum, look!"

The front said "Plum and Boy." I broke open the seal, and inside was the following:

Dear Boys,

A Recipe for an Open Mind

4 pounds of onion roots
Wild basil to taste
Chopped carrots
Fresh spring water, two or three quarts
Tuber bullion in appropriate quantity
Mushrooms from the wide world (Westwoods, Northern Territory), sautéed in wild goat butter
Cook over an open flame in the open air (do not boil)
Serves all willing to let their senses wander . . .
Kosher salt and freshly ground black pepper to taste

Yours,
W. Bigfoot

p.s. Thanks for the head start!

Plum cooks me Walt's soup every year on my birthday, and we travel back to the open minds of our fourteenth year. And when we hear about encounters with Bigfoot in the Westwoods, east of North Camp, we believe them, and wonder what the lucky hiker, or lumberman, or tracker had for supper, and if Walt served them dessert.

11. Organ

Right lower quadrant abdominal pain, fever, vomiting, and no appetite means you're off to the hospital to have your appendix out. I'm told it's a worthless organ—a holdover from our primitive days, meant for digesting raw mammoth on a stick. Now it's a cash cow for otherwise idle general surgeons.

As the anesthesia wore off I batted my eyes, trying to clear pentobarbital cobwebs from my brain.

"How was it, Boy? Did you meet our maker? Is there really a bright light after all?"

Plum was sitting next to my bed.

"Why are you here, Plum? I thought this was supposed to be the recovery room, where I could relax for a few minutes with young nurses and my new scar!" More powerful than any anesthesia, my 15-year-olds hormones were kicking back in strong, post-op.

"Well Boy, I'm here to cheer you up."

Just then my surgeon, Dr. Thomas Reed, ambled up to my bed, to see that everything left of me was in order. He was a pale-faced gentleman, with a prominent lower jaw and a receding hairline. His gut protruded about eighteen inches out of sky-blue scrubs, the result of too much operating room time over the past twenty-two years, or perhaps too few walks out in the air with the rest of us. But I didn't discount his expertise. Somebody has to take appendixes out.

"We took a nice pocket of pus out of you today," he said. (Surgeons, always full of charm.) "You'll be on your feet before you know it. Take it easy on that scar for a month or two. And stay away from my daughter, or I'll have you back here to remove your—"

"Ok, I get the get the point. Say hello to Nicole for us, and tell her we miss her," I added with a grin. Nicole Reed was Dr. Reed's youngest daughter, a honey-pie a couple of years younger than us, still trapped in junior high. Plum and I were looking forward to her high school debut.

"Don't test me, Boy. I've got scalpels for plenty of other procedures," Dr. Reed said on his way out. But then Plum leaned over, and whispered into my ear.

"One more thing," I yelled, stopping Dr. Reed in his tracks. "Can I have it?"

"What?"

"My appendix. Can I have the organ?"

"You want your appendix?"

"Yes sir, very much so, sir. Thank you."

"I'll see what I can do. It's yours, after all."

Over the next few days, I endured two annoying roommates. One was a self-proclaimed intellectual from Haverford, who had undergone an emergency splenectomy. The other was a gassy plumber with a partial small bowel resection.

"This place is really snatching up vital organs," Plum commented.

"They're taking sick organs out of people, Plum. You make it sound like the invasion of the organ snatchers."

"I just call it as I see it. And don't get me wrong, Boy, I think it's the wave of the future."

"What is?"

"Organ removal. Organ removal is the wave of the future! I guarantee it!"

Here we go again.

"That's right. In the future, all of us are going to have our organs removed one by one. Only we're not going to be stupid, and wait until they're infected, or failing, or riddled with tumors. We're going to remove them when they're healthy."

"Plum, what goes on in your head? Why would anyone remove a healthy organ? IT'S HEALTHY. Get it!"

"By the time an appendix needs out, it's too late. The rest of the body is hurting. Right? Or have you seen someone with kidney failure on dialysis? It's not pretty. What I'm proposing is that we take people's organs out on a proper timetable, modeled on the actuarial of when those organs typically go south. But here's the kicker. We'll replace them with shiny mechanical ones. Probably titanium."

"I can see it now, Plum. A middle-aged accountant rolls up to the emergency department window. 'Could you please remove my gallbladder, and my adenoids, while you're at it?' The person running the cash register replies, 'Certainly, sir. That will be $2,600 for the gallbladder, and $500 for your adenoids. Thank you, and come again soon.'"

"Do I detect sarcasm?"

"All right," I said, "get to the specifics. When does the appendix go?"

"Early, obviously," he said. "That's too easy; it's worthless anyway."

"The heart?"

"That's better. I'd say about forty. No one has heart attacks before then."

"Pancreas?"

"Fifty-three," he said quickly, even though you actually need your pancreas—well, Plum was no doctor.

"Brain?"

"Well, some people should have their brains removed right from the start, but my guess is that the natural lifespan of a human brain is about seventy-five years. After that, it's due for a tune-up, at the very least."

"And where are you going to get all these mechanical hearts, brains and pancrei?"

"I'm all about the theory, Boy. We're scientists. Leave the specifics to the engineers."

I was satisfied.

The next time I saw Dr. Reed, he had a vial filled with thick-brownish liquid in his hand.

"Good news, Boy. I'm discharging you today. And here's your appendix!" He put the vial down on the bedside table. My appendix was bobbing in it.

After Dr. Reed had left, Plum snatched up the vial, putting his close investigative eye on that good-for-nothing-fibrous-swollen-cecal-appendage that had made me vomit just five days before.

"Not much to it is, is there? Just a dab of flesh waiting for an infection."

"That's about the sum of it, Plum. Let me have a look."

Looking at one's own appendix is a little like . . . actually, there's nothing that comes to mind. But it did turn my stomach a little, so I gave the vial back to Plum.

"Here, keep this for me. I'll check on it from time to time. But let's keep this a private affair, please."

"No problem. I understand completely."

Plum smiled.

I was released on a Saturday afternoon, so I had the weekend to recover before returning to school. My mother was very understanding about my level of general discomfort. She told my dad that I should stay home for the better part of the week. Dad grumbled.

"When I was a boy, we went back to school the same day they took our appendices out."

"Nonsense!" Mother snapped. "When you were a boy, they just left your appendix in to explode. Boy's been through plenty. A day or two away from school isn't going to hurt him."

Little did I know.

On Wednesday morning I felt much better than expected. I wasn't the kind of kid who liked to miss school even if I had a reason. I liked it actually. So I threw on some jeans and a t-shirt, and headed school. I got a curious glance or two from some girls on the number two bus, but I didn't make anything out of it. Girls were strange as it was. Odd, though—Plum was nowhere to be seen.

I was still fairly tender, so I did a walking-on-egg-shells-to-protect-my-yolk kind of traveling. If I had paid any attention at all, I would have noticed that everyone was staring at me. And I certainly knew when entering homeroom that it was absolutely silent, with all eyes were turned on me.

"What is it?" I asked. "What are you people looking at? What's wrong with you?"

Though a whisper or two slipped out, nearly everyone held their tongues. Only when I got to my desk did a longtime row mate let me in on the reason for all the increased attention.

"Your kid brother's been walking around with your kidney."

"What?"

Brother must have stolen it from Plum.

"He's got it in a bottle, and people are paying him two dollars each just to see it."

"That's not my kidney, it's my appendix."

"Whatever. It's still grossing everyone out. At least it was, until—"

"Until what?" I asked, fearing the worst.

"Until Mr. Schroder took it from him in study hall."

"OH GOD!"

Mr. Schroder was a red-faced-lunatic biology teacher who took pleasure in embarrassing us during sex ed class. What would become of my appendix in his hands? Well I was certainly going to find out soon. Plum and I had honors biology with him in third period. And wait until I got my hands on Plum!

First and second periods couldn't have passed more slowly. When that third bell rang, I ran—hobbled—to room 207, where Plum and I would meet again over my poor over-exposed appendix. I got to the room nearly last. All of the principal players were waiting for me, including the organ, which was sitting on Mr. Schroder's desk at the front of the class. Anyone who hadn't had a sneak preview on Monday or Tuesday was clearly getting an eyeful now.

"I'm glad the rest of you could join us, Boy," Mr. Schroder began. Take a seat there, next to your appendix. Class, this is an appendix—not a kidney, as some of you have been led to believe. Its purpose . . ."

Schroder's lecture faded into black as I tried to meet Plum's eyes so that I could turn him to stone. After about twenty minutes, he looked over, and I gave him that look. He gave me his best *oops* glance back, and handed me an envelope under the table.

"What's this?"

"Two hundred dollars from your appendix fund."

As I had so many times before, and I've had to so many times since, I shook my head.

"I didn't ask for this!"

"I know. That's what makes it such a wonderful gesture on my part."

I was in a trance for our entire Biology class and the first thing I remember hearing was, "and that is why each of you is born with an appendix, and why Boy doesn't have one today." Schroder's lecture ended right when the bell rang, signaling the end of third period. We made for the door, but Schroder got me by the collar. "Boy, I just wanted to thank you for being so supportive of public education. If you have anything else to contribute to my biology class, I'll be happy to put you in my lesson plan again next week."

Far down the hall, away from our freakish biology teacher, I let Plum have it.

"How could you let my appendix circulate? That thing was inside of me! Now everyone is seeing it!"

"Boy, first of all I didn't give it to Schroder. Your rat brother did. Second, only his honors biology classes have anatomy, so everyone will not be seeing your appendix. And third, WHO CARES? You're a star! Ask anyone. They've been talking about you for the past 48 hours—since your organ came to their attention."

"Who?" I asked. "Who thinks I'm a star?"

"The girls, you fool! The girls! Don't you see how they're staring at you?"

He was right. As we walked down the hall, every fifteen-year old girl was making eyes at me like I had walked on the moon!

"But why, Plum? Why are these crazy girls interested in me now? They never were before."

"Because girls love a boy with guts. And they've actually seen yours."

Plum was right. Somehow the public display of my appendix had vaulted me into extreme, though short-lived, popularity among the stranger sex. No fewer than six of the cutest girls in our biology class asked if they could carry my books. Who was I to say no? I let them take turns.

Once Plum and I were alone again, I asked him once more why there'd been such a positive reaction to the public display of my appendix.

"Because people love visceral moments in life, Boy. And your bottled body part was an extreme example of exactly that, a visceral moment. And besides, when it comes to the opposite sex, forget your brain and trust your guts. They will lead you to love every time."

12. The Adventure of Y

"Boy," Plum began, sitting across from me in our high school physics class, while Mr. Taylor, oblivious to interruption, was hard at work trying to make sense out of centripetal force, "hard-core psychosis or schizophrenia don't worry me. It's the semi-psychotic behavior of the everyday-seemingly-normal-all-American that makes my skin crawl."

"Plum, are you saying that Aunt Erma's conversations with St. Jerome don't bother you?"

"Well I wouldn't say that the Aunt Ermas of the world make me comfortable, but she's a known nut, so at least I can understand her. She believes St. Jerome is talking to her. Ask her why he is talking to her and she'll tell you. It means something to her. It's the world's blind followers who scare me. You want to know insane, I'll tell you! Staying at a red light in the middle of the night, when no one else is around—that's insane! Driving with the arrows in an empty parking lot—that's insane too!"

"You have a lot of automotive angst, Plum," I said, baiting him. "Is that all that's insane in the world?"

"No, Boy," he said with a smile. "Those are just two examples, there are plenty more."

"For instance?"

"Racists are insane. So is someone who tells you guns are good, a constitutional American right. They kill people!"

"And waterfowl!" I had interrupted. "Sorry, go on," I said.

"People who tell you that they love you before getting to know you are insane, and that's a bad one, Boy. I'm warning you! Things can get very scary quite quickly. People who hate you without knowing you are equally insane. Just meaner."

I kept encouraging him. "Okay, fast lovers and haters. Are they the only insane ones?"

"Do you mean besides red light stoppers and arrow followers? No, they're not all. People who pick up their dog's bowel movements in the woods are pretty insane. People who mow their lawns more than once a week after September fifteenth need a good psychiatrist. Compulsive rakers are the worst, though. Give me a man who rakes his lawn three times a week, and I'll show you someone ready for a kill-crazy rampage."

I started worrying right then, thinking about Dr. Griffin, our aging next door neighbor, who raked his maple leaves daily into neat piles between our properties.

"Who else?"

"The hair transplant community is insane! In my experience, I've found bald people generally much better adjusted than the average Joe. But give a bald guy a new plug or two on his brow and beware!

"And twins tend to be completely insane. I understand that, though. With two identical people running around the planet, how could you possibly hope for sanity? 'Hi, this is my brother Bob. He looks, acts, smells, talks, and thinks like me, but we're really very different people deep down inside!' Go figure. Anyone who can see himself without a mirror can hardly be expected to maintain his sanity."

He had a point.

"Most assembly line workers go insane gradually. Anyone who has to do the same thing constantly, for whatever reason, is a candidate. Watch for that glazed look in the eyes of the sixty-something year old who has proudly-been-on-the-job-doing-his-duty in a perverted countdown to retirement for forty years."

"Might as well hand him a rake."

"Exactly!"

"Well, who isn't insane, Plum? Who doesn't go mad?"

"Just one person, Boy. The adventurer! The adventurer is alive and breathing every day, until fate throws him from the train. He's sane, even if he falls off of a cliff to prove it. In fact, I'll go you one better. Show me someone society disapproves of, criminals notwithstanding, and I'll show you an intact mind."

That got me thinking.

"You see, Boy, it's all about control. Society wants to control everything, and especially itself, so it creates one thousand and two rules to follow. Break a rule, and you're an outsider; break two, and you're a rebel. Three rules means you're a criminal, and society locks you up. I hope it chokes.

Follow all of the rules, and you're a solid citizen, you're rewarded. Just never ask them Y. Y is the way to trouble!"

"I don't understand. What exactly is the problem?"

The Idea Man

"Here's the problem, Boy. Following rules means abandoning thought, the thinking process. You must turn your mind off, check your brain at the door, and sit down quietly. You can't ask any questions. 'Do your job the way I say, because that's the way things work!' Insanity guaranteed!"

"Now the adventurer is the sane one," Plum continued, "and make no mistake, we can all be adventurers. Even if we pass on cliff-diving. In fact, only one adventure's required to save your mind. The Adventure of Y. Choose this, and you've chosen a life lived insanity-free."

I had heard a lot of interesting, but obtuse and confused ideas come out of Plum's mouth, but the Adventure of Y was the most confused idea yet. For years we had been absolutely of the same mind, but now I didn't know what he was talking about. I wondered if we were growing apart, and it worried me.

"What is it, Plum? This Adventure of Y?

"It's your ticket to real living Boy, the key to our shackles."

Sounds like trouble, I thought.

"It is trouble," Plum replied. "But it's the only way to live. Skip the Adventure of Y and you've skipped life, let it pass you by."

"Yes, what the heck is it!"

"I keep telling you, Boy! The Adventure of Y is the key to the shackles strapped onto a boy's ankles when he starts first grade and learns that the world is full of rules, with too little naptime. The Adventure of Y is that first moment that you decide as an individual (he spoke that word very loudly, to get my complete attention) to discover what's really going on. You're six, and almost everyone is a huge towering authority figure, armed with a list of rules ready to keep you from letting your mind wander. Don't listen to them, Boy. Not when you're six, or sixty-six, or one hundred and sixty-six.

Take Y and run with it. Run with Y, as fast and hard, and as far as you can. Then run some more!"

"But what is it, Plum? What is the Adventure of Y made of? How will I know it when I see it?"

A calm came over him.

"When nothing makes sense, and the world around you tells you what to do 'just because,' don't do it! Ask yourself Y. Y me? And Y now?"

Something in his voice made me think that this would be his last advice for a long time. And I began to feel lonely.

"When you ask Y, you'll have embarked on the Adventure of Y, the real journey in this world. And you might even be setting the stage for the one adventure that's even more fulfilling than the adventure of Y itself."

"And what's that, Plum?" I felt a smile breaking out across my being again, as I came back in touch with my best and closest friend's ideas. "What could that possibly be?"

Plum smiled.

"The Adventure of Y not."

13. In Between

Then one day he was gone. Plum. Without a trace—out of sight, but never out of mind.

It happened at the end our first summer after graduating from high school. We had done well, even though no one had really understood the workings of our minds. Plum's eccentricities were legendary, and I was his confidant. We were outsiders in an inside game.

I finished near the top of the class, and was "on my way"—or so said the successful members of Seasoncreek. Who cares at that age, I wonder? Who cares now? Still, we had seemed different, and since no community has ever existed where a couple of creative trouble-making kids weren't watched closely, we were monitored to an extreme. As an eighteen year old, going away was everything to me—whenever and however, but probably by car. So I went on my way to college. And Plum disappeared.

College passed like the blink meant to keep winter air out of the eyes—a perfect union of passionate friendships, intellectual growth, and emotional disarray. I lived in that great place for four years. New friends gathered—Lucy White and Evans, the Dreamer, the Wild Turk, Q, and Camacho.

Medical school came next, passing even faster than college, half a blink, a wink. Everyone asks, of course, but I'm actually not sure why I became a doctor. It's a rather boring question, though perhaps no more boring than my answer. At the time it didn't occur to me to do anything else. That's all.

To this day I'm torn about growing up. Most people seem in favor of it, but not me. I liked my boyhood self, so why would I want to change? This period of my life was strangely lacking in inspiration. No spirit moved me. Plum might say, "Looking back now, it wasn't a mistake then," but as far as reasons for decisions go, it might have helped to have some. Everyone said I'd make a good doctor, so I became one. Plum's favorite adventure. Y not?

Not.

Ten years passed before I moved back to Seasoncreek. I had come home for the holidays, of course, to see my family and some of the close friends I had accumulated while "growing up." They did exist, even if I haven't said much about them—Malcolm, AD, Purple Hayes, Fig, Warrington, and Slow Roberts.

I returned with the lines of my life so tight and twisted that I didn't know if I was the same Boy who had left a decade before. Maybe someone could tell me, but who? Not my mother. I was still her baby boy: I hadn't changed since I was six. Only one person could have straightened this matter out for me. But Plum had gone away, and hadn't come back at all. My going away to college had been predictable. Plum's vanishing into thin air was a complete mystery. I didn't know where, or even if he was. It was hard to take.

Once back in Seasoncreek, a normal life came quickly. I married a great girl, bought a small one-story building on Main Street, and hung my name above the door.

The Idea Man

But something was missing.

The building was solid red brick, with only five rooms of any consequence. The waiting room had two uncomfortable wooden benches and a coat rack. A second room held patient records, and Hilda Pumpkin, my nurse/office manager. She had a huge walnut desk, cluttered and covered with yellow sticky notes.

"Call Mr. Hollander to schedule his prostate exam."

"Need more tongue depressors."

Pumpkin kept me afloat. I'll tell you more about her later if I get the chance.

There was a bathroom of course. And of course, there was my office/exam room. I had a desk, and plenty of books, filled with horrifically complex material devoted to the spleen, pancreas, kidneys, and liver. There was an exam table with a small cupboard beside it, holding my stethoscope, ophthalmoscope, otoscope, and other scopes. The room also had two oversized leather chairs to sit on, but usually only one person to sit. Me.

Number five? A tiny alcove attached to my office, just waiting for someone to hide in. Ultimately it became quite an important little space. And there you have it—a perfectly adequate environment for a small-town-country-medical-practice, and a young doctor who liked to daydream.

I spent my first six months wading through the strange and mundane medical histories of Seasoncreek. The patients seemed to take to me. I suppose they liked to have the local Boy back in town, but I was also a fairly agreeable listener when they trotted out personal hypotheses about their ailments.

They liked this. When Mrs. Roswell told me "Consumption" was worse on days that the competitive bridge club (the CBC) met outdoors near her rosebushes, who was I to disagree? I moved the game to an airy porch. And if Mr. Hennessey's urine was purple because of the vegetables that his wife served, I wasn't going to change his mind—just his taste for beets and bok choi. Simply put, then, my Seasoncreek clientele and I were getting on splendidly. I was content, but somehow lonely.

Then one day, I was just finishing working Mr. Rodgers up for a facial tic when Pumpkin knocked.

"Dr. Boy," she yelled through the door. At least three decades older than me, she insisted on using my first name and my title simultaneously. "Your carpet is here."

"My what?"

"Rug! The delivery people are here, and they want to know where to put it."

I opened the door.

"Put it? I don't know why they brought it. I didn't order a carpet."

"Well they're here with one," she replied, clearly happy that I was in some sort of bind. She was a bit devious, in a great-auntie kind of way. This might provide her with some enjoyment.

In front of me were two men, hunched over under the weight of a huge oriental rug. It was so big that even rolled up they could barely get it into my exam room.

"I didn't order that thing," I said. "Are you sure you have the right building?"

One of the men cut me off in mid-sentence.

"I know where I am, and I know that you didn't order this faraway, wonderful, fabulous, carpet monstrosity straight from the Near-East. It's a present!"

"A present? From whom?"

They dropped the rug in the center of my office and straightened up. One guy left. The other one stared me in the face. As his shag of wildish hair parted, my jaw

The Idea Man

dropped. The gleam of Larry Plum's boyhood eyes was shining out of an adult Plum face.

"When did you…" I stammered at my best friend in the world.

"Just now Dr. Boy, I just got home."

Plum said the word "doctor" with three parts sarcasm, two parts disbelief, and one part big brotherly pride.

"Seeing you and unloading this rug were priorities one and two."

"Well, where the heck have you been?"

My next questions would haven been, "And what the heck have you been doing? Weaving rugs?" But Plum as always read my mind.

"I've been everywhere and nowhere new at all. And I didn't weave this one. I traded for it on a dig in East Africa— my rights to two square meters full of Australopithecine forearms for this magnificent 17th century Ottoman eschudo. When I heard that you had an office where we would be charting out the future, I figured the carpet might help bring our ideas out. What's one early hominid bone more or less anyway?"

And that's how Larry Plum dropped back into my life. Ten years to a thirty year old seems like a millennium to, well, three millennia. But not a thing had changed between us. That's the definition of friendship. And it was even a nice rug.

I cancelled my appointments. We spent the rest of that afternoon lying on the newly-carpeted floor. My office had become a home. And once again, my mind began to whirl.

14. A Dialogue

After my family had retired one winter night, Plum joined me the study for a whisky in front of the fire. It was the end of January. In our youth, frozen Seasoncreek was a joy. Now it chilled us to the bone, but the fire helped.

We each had a comfortable chair we favored. Plum's chair faced the fireplace; mine was behind a desk buried underneath piles of medical journals and scraps of paper meant to serve as important reminders, most forever unheeded.

I stirred the fire, then planted myself behind the desk, shuffling some of the papers out of a sense of duty, habit, and guilt. Finally, I waded into the conversation Plum and I needed to have, though I didn't yet know what it would be about.

"Why so quiet at dinner, Plum? I've never known you to keep your ideas to yourself."

ZZZZzzzzzz. ZZZZzzzzzz. ZZZZzzzzzz.

Snoring loudly from the depths of his leather chair, perched on the edge of the blazing fire, Plum tossed and turned violently in his sleep. We had only been in the room for three minutes, and he was out cold. He must have been exhausted, but he wasn't a restful sight. His brow furrowed and his ears twitched, as sweat dripped from him. His arms flailed around, as if he was warding off demons.

This went on for about an hour and a half. Of agony for him, I guessed, and certainly for me. It's hard to watch that kind of torment in your best friend. Then suddenly he sprang straight up out of his chair and faced me, soaked from his bad dream.

"What if I haven't got one, Boy? What if I never had? What if they don't even exist!" He collapsed back into his chair, his head in his hands.

What could one say to this?

"What if you haven't got what? Plum, you were having a nightmare."

From between his fingers, he mumbled, "awful shame" and "who's to blame?" He was still half asleep.

"Plum, snap out of it! Speak up! What's a shame? Who's to blame? Tell me what's on your mind!"

"No shame or blame, it's my middle name! I haven't got one, Boy, and what if I never did? What if it never was? I'm not sure about anything anymore!"

Plum had been thinking quite a lot lately—more than usual even for him. Don't think too much, if you can help it.

"Plum, what do you mean middle names don't exist? That's crazy!"

"How do you know, Boy? What makes you so sure middle names exist! What is a middle name? Can you see one? Feel one?"

"No, I guess not, Plum. But they exist. I'm certain of that."

"I'm inclined to agree with you, Boy, after what the master taught me. I know middle names exist for most people, but I'm not so sure about me. It's pretty darn hard to prove anything exists, let alone something like a middle name. You can't smell a middle name."

Something had happened to Plum during his time away that kicked his mind into an even higher gear than before. He had become more philosophical, while I became medically practical—some might even say dull. I envied him.

But I was still confused about this middle name quandary, so I asked him to explain it to me one day. And he did.

"Not long ago, Plum said, "I was sitting on the steps of the Parthenon, wondering how I had traveled so far and seen so many things, but hadn't found my middle name. This seemed impossible. Surely I should have tripped over it somewhere along the way."

"Why the Parthenon, Plum? What took you there?"

"They say that the Greeks built the Parthenon for Athena, the Goddess of Wisdom, so I was hoping that some might rub off on me. It was a dumb idea, I guess— but there was a nice coffee shop, and lots of interesting Greeks. So I stayed. Every morning I climbed up the steps, and tried to imagine what it was like in the 5th Century B.C. when the Parthenon was built, with all the great epistemologists wandering around, proving this and that to people. That's when it occurred to me that maybe middle names don't exist at all, that maybe they are just a part of an imaginary world. Perhaps then I never had a middle name to lose! What would Plato say?"

"I don't know Plum, what would Plato say?"

"Funny you should ask, Boy, because I asked him myself last month, and he said . . . "

"You talked to Plato?" Plum had gone mad.

The Idea Man

"Yes. In a dream on the steps of the Acropolis—well, I guess it was a dream. One afternoon I was sitting on the marble stairs when an ancient, wrinkled Greek man carrying at least ten thick books walked past me. He was completely bald on top, and he had an enormously long white beard that touched the ground where it came to a point five feet beneath his chin. If his posture had been better, he wouldn't have stepped on his beard, tripped himself, and came crashing to the ground. Books flew in every direction!

"What happened then, Plum? Just tell me what happened."

"I approached the old man, and helped him pick up the scattered books. 'Hello sir. My name is Lawrence Plum, but my friend, Boy, calls me Plum. Are you okay?'

"The old man creaked as he straightened upright. 'Yes son, I'm fine, thank you. My name is Plato, but my teacher Socrates calls me the Master. How can I help you?'

'Master, how does anyone know anything.'

'Could you please be a little more specific? I have a class to teach, so I'm on a tight schedule here.'

'Okay. I've always thought I lost my middle name, but now I'm afraid that it never actually existed.'

'This is an area I haven't addressed yet. Let me then ask you something. Are some people ashamed of their middle names?'

'Of course,'

"Now let me ask you something else. Are some people proud of their middle names?

'Certainly.'

'In fact, Plum, don't some people prefer to be known to the world by their middle names?'

'I suppose so. But what does all of this mean, Plato?'

'How therefore can someone be ashamed or proud of something that doesn't exist? And further, how could someone be known by a figment of the imagination?'

'They couldn't be.'

'Exactly. So you see, Plum, your soul knows your middle name.'

'What?'

'Everyone's middle names must be related to their ideal middle name.'

'What?'

'Behind the changing veil of everyday appearances there is an eternal, immutable reality of ideal forms. That is where the ideal middle name dwells. Whether you like it or not, your soul knows that middle name. You just can't remember it.'

'But—'

'Traveling the path of the philosopher requires the casting away of all appearances. This is the journey toward what is true. This is the journey you must take to find your own middle name, to see what your soul already knows.'

Plum then panicked. His soul may know his middle name, but what if he was without a soul? So he fought back.

'Plato, if you're so sure about all of this, then what does your soul tell you about your middle name?'

Plato paused. He had of course never pondered his own middle name before. Everyone had always just called him Plato. What was his own middle name?

'Well, I, I, I—' The Master stuttered as he tried to pull his middle name from the recesses of his own soul.

"Well, Plato of Athens, your middle name is *of*. A preposition! What do you make of that!'

Plato smiled sympathetically.

'Yes, Plum, my middle name may be *of*. I will think about that. But taking your frustrations out on me will not help you in your quest for the truth."

'I know. I'm sorry,' Plum said, and Plato accepted Plum's apology completely.

'Remember, Plum, as a part of eternal reality, your soul is omniscient, since memory is always a recollection of experience. Chase down those moments veering closest to your middle name, and you will find what you seek. You, Larry Plum, will find your middle name.'

'I will continue my search. Thank you, Master.'

'Good boy.'
Plato walked away, wiping his brow.

Plum fixed his eyes on me and asked me what I thought about his encounter with the master. This was an odd moment. Everything Plum told me that Plato had said fit perfectly with the Dialogues of Plato. I knew. I'd read them. Plum might as well have been a Socratic student. But what did it matter, anyway? The truth was in the telling—or in the looking now, I suppose.

"So what now, Plum? Where do we go next?"

"I guess we search wherever my soul takes us."

"That could be anywhere, Plum! That could take forever!"

"Exactly." He smiled. "But what is life if not a search for yourself?" And I realized that adventure lay ahead once more.

"So why were you having nightmares, Plum?"

"Because it's terrifying to search for yourself. You never know what you might not find!"

15. Toe 6

Months passed. Plum settled comfortably into the previously neglected alcove, that half-a-room attached to my office. This allowed for privacy for both me and my patients, but also gave me the chance to rekindle the dialogue with Plum that had defined my childhood. The rug had also made a difference. My office now felt like a home.

"Plum," I said, "do you feel that things are going according to plan?"

"I don't have a plan, Boy," he said, poking his head through the alcove door, "but if I had one, I'm guessing that nothing would go or come according to it. What's your problem, Boy? You seem a trifle troubled."

"I am. Twelve years have come and gone without a major incident. I set out to become a doctor, to create a good life, and it happened—no trouble at all!"

I was raising my voice.

"And that troubles you?" Plum asked as empathetically as he could, even though empathy wasn't Plum's forte.

"Yes! Before you disappeared, our life was one strange happening after another. Commotion compounding misunderstanding! Now it's all so predictable."

Plum sat down across from me in his comfortable, leather throne.

"I can see how that would bother you, Boy. You're missing the conflict that a soul needs, but like good luck, there's only so much chaos to go around. You'll have to wait your turn, I'm afraid. But take heart. I'm certain that uncertainty will creep back into your life soon."

"How do you know, Plum? How can you be sure?"

"Because Bower proved it to me a few years ago, just off the coast of the Netherlands Antilles." And then he told me this tale.

Bower was a handsome lad, somewhere between six and seven feet. Because he was so tall, and by any woman's account good looking, when he finished school and decided to carve out a sensible, materialistic existence in the "real world," as he called it, success came easily. His brain was above average on most days, and bankers took to him. Bower had no objection to the money this profession brought, so he became one.

Bower became a wealthy banker-bachelor in no time at all, and a married man in practically less. Mrs. Bower, the most beautiful woman in his entire county, loved Bower's height and good looks and money. She even liked his office at the bank, where he spent the majority of his time when he wasn't at The Club. I really don't know anything else about Mrs. Bower, other than she was beautiful. To be honest, that's also about all that Bower knew about her too. But he was OK with that.

Bower's life was going splendidly. One morning he even woke up, turned to his splendid wife, and said, 'My life is going splendidly.' He was twenty-six and one half years old.

The Idea Man

"Soon I'll be president of the bank and we'll be really rich. You'll get pregnant, and we'll have a tall son who will think highly of me just like everyone else does."

Bower's beautiful wife smiled at the thought.

"And after that," he continued, "things will only get better, because my job will get better and better, and I'll still be tall and you will still be beautiful."

Bower was certain about his life's course, and she was too.

Not so many weeks later, Bower was getting ready for his usual Wednesday at the bank, making money. He had just taken a long, steamy shower in his marble bathroom—a bathroom with many mirrors that fogged up completely when the hot water was on. In his usual preoccupied way, Bower washed and dried himself. Then he began to shave.

The mirror in handsome, tall Bower's marble bathroom was so covered with steam that he had to put down his straight razor on several occasions, and wipe the mirror with a monogrammed towel. Toward the end of his shave, Bower was wiping the shower fog off the mirror yet again when he accidentally-unpredictably knocked his razor off of the sink, and onto the floor next to his right foot. Relieved that he hadn't cut himself, he bent over to pick the razor up.

That's when he noticed that he had grown a sixth toe on his right foot—a stubby clone of the fifth pinky toe, which he already considered utterly useless.

He blinked a few times, double vision was to blame, but the sixth toe was still there— functional, pink, and perfect. Cutting off that disturbing new toe wasn't the solution, and Bower was no surgeon and small toes really bleed (I don't need to elaborate, do I).

92

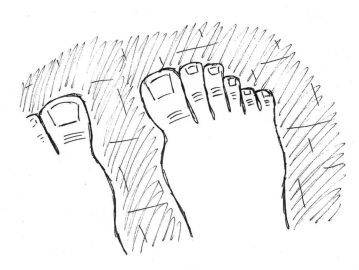

Flustered and flummoxed, Bower did however manage to pull himself together and get to work. Unfortunately, none of Bower's expensive Italian shoes would accommodate the sixth toe, so he was forced to wear old broken-in running shoes to the bank. This really upset him, mostly because Bower did not want to draw any attention to his new problem, and wearing running shoes to work was a sure way to do just that. Dressed for a formal jog, Bower was in a fix.

He resolved to go about his day as though he hadn't grown a sixth toe on his right foot. He pretended that he still had only five toes, and that he was wearing expensive Italian shoes. But as his meetings approached, he lost his nerve.

"How can I go to my meetings in running shoes?"

So he canceled his meetings, and went home sick. Six toe sick. The next day came and went. Bower stayed home; his wife didn't notice.

The Idea Man

By the following week, Bower had missed so many banking meetings that ten-toed Mike, his slightly shorter and less handsome rival at the bank, rose above him in banker favor. This was a big dilemma. The senior bankers wanted an explanation from their favorite son, but would they take eleven toes for an answer?

They're good people, Bower thought, totally overestimating them. They will understand.

So he decided to come clean. The truth about the toe would be exposed.

"Mr. Bower, I understand you can explain your recent failings on the job," the venerable bank president said to him.

"Yes sir. You see, I've grown a sixth toe on my right foot, and it has made me lose my focus."

Ah, the relief! He had said it. Now they could all move on, resume banking. He was sure he could get new shoes, tailored to meet his needs.

"You're fired!"

So Bower lost his job, and stopped shaving regularly, thanks to sixth toe depression. He also quickly lost his gentlemanly good looks—stooped a little, seemed shorter—made less money (basically his severance package) and lost his beautiful wife, who really wasn't anything special anyway—just beautiful.

Then Bower met Plum, on a boat just off the coast of the Netherlands Antilles. I assumed Bower must have been miserable, recounting the loss of his career, money, wife, even height and good looks—and all because of his newfound toe. I was totally wrong. Bower actually told Plum that he felt saved, not lost. I didn't understand that. His life was upside down, inside out. From outside, all seemed lost.

"Boy," Plum said, "you're right about loss. Bower lost his old life, but he found a new one—one with 'wind in his hair and water between his toes'—all eleven of them, as he put it. And he hadn't planned any of it. Change came without warning."

"So why are you telling me about Bower and his life turned upside down?"

"Because uncertainty is as certain as certain can be. You say your life is without ripples, without conflict. Change will come like a sixth toe—when you don't expect it, but absolutely when you need it."

"And what happened to Bower?"

"You mean how did his life turn out? It turned out to be his."

I liked the sound of that. And I looked down at my own feet, just to see if my toes were still keeping the same company.

16. Angeland

"Where do angels come from, Boy?" Plum asked me one day as we walked between the rows of gravestones at Seasoncreek's cemetery—Mathews, Zagon, Miranda, Gregor, Piker, Jenkins, Maddox, Ives, Demsky, Feynman, Whitcomb, English, Block, Buckstead, Javar, Osterman, Evans, Bloom, Gabbard, Unlu, Basson, Hobbs, McCune, Abrahams—searching for relatives long ago dead.

"I don't think they come from heaven," he continued. "What sense would that make? Going there to come back here, just to help us get up there!"

He had lost me.

"Well Boy, what do you think? Where do the angels come from?"

"I don't even know if I believe in angels, so how on Earth can I tell you where they live? Probably Angeland," I added sarcastically.

There was a long pause from my friend, then his ideas began to flow.

Angeland

"Angeland. Yes, that's it. They must have land—probably swimming in it, after all the good they've done.

"Let me guess Plum, Angels get property as payment from—"

"That's right. God!" he answered. "They're not Buddhists, they're angels! And don't give me that look, Boy. Why not Angeland? They must still have some material needs. Surely it's not all wings and harps up there."

"I don't think it's only wings or harps because I doubt angels exist at all. And they certainly don't live on property awarded by God! They 'live' in an imaginary world of hope and miracles. We create angels because we need to believe in something, so everything's not just chaos and uncertainty—random existence in a random Universe!" Now he was looking at, instead of staring beyond, me.

"Wow! Medicine has done a number on you, Boy. When did hope and miracles become figments of people's imagination?"

"Sometime during internship, when I watched one person after another suffer and die, from cancer, or from car accidents, drugs, or heart attacks thirty years before their fat time, Plum! That's when my angels flew away!"

He considered the expression of pain and suffering on my face. I meant what I was saying, and he knew it.

"Boy, watching those people die and suffer was horrible. But that can't mean that your angels are gone. They're just asleep, waiting for the right time to wake up. There's a time for everyone's angels."

"Plum, after seeing so much pain, I don't believe in them."

"Who ever said that angels are meant to take pain away? Maybe their job is to bring our pain to us, then help us survive it."

97

"What are you talking about, Plum? Angels creating pain and not stopping it? What devil-angels are these?" His concept of the divine confused me.

"What I'm saying, my friend, is angels keep us on track, from getting too lost when the night is black. Finding your angel, is like me finding my middle name. Without them, we're incomplete."

"So do you and I have an angel, Plum, to keep us on track?"

"Absolutely."

"Who?"

"Joseph Kunch," he said, with a certainty that seemed completely inappropriate to the question.

"You mean great-grandpa Joe Kunch, who hung himself from our apple tree out back?"

"Yes, hanging-Grandpa-Joe is one of our angels. There are others, but he's definitely one of them."

"How do you know? Where is he? And what others?"

"He's not still in the apple tree, if that's your question, Boy."

"Of course not, we chopped that tree down two summers ago, didn't we?"

"Exactly!" he shot back, "he's not in the apple tree. He's all around us, keeping us away from orchards and other hazardous fruit trees."

"Do you really believe in angels, Plum, or are you just messing around?"

"I do," he replied, "and I've even met one recently."

"Where and when exactly did that meeting take place?"

"Upstate New York—last summer. Only I didn't realize at the time that she was an angel. She's dead now, or gone anyhow. It's a tricky business describing an angel's comings and goings."

"Plum, who are you talking about. What angel do you know from New York?"

"Jo Anne."

"Who?"

"Jo Anne!"

"Aunt Jo Anne who married Uncle Jimmy? Her?" I was very confused. "Plum I knew Jo Anne. What makes you think she was an angel? She was nice, but just another—"

"Angel! Boy, she was OBVIOUSLY an angel. Think about Jo Anne, remember how she came and went from Uncle Jimmy's life, and you'll understand. Don't make me prove it to you."

So I thought their story through in my mind, and things became clear.

Jimmy was smart his whole life, but his brains were all bottled up inside of him. Pressurized—that's what MIT can do to a bright young man! By the time he was thirty, he had studied so much that he'd missed the first wave of girls. (They do come in waves, but that's another story.) When he turned forty, we were all sure he would be an intellectual-bachelor for the rest of his life. At forty-seven, he seemed to be the definition of a man alone. Then smart Jimmy announced that he was marrying the beautiful and sweet Jo Anne. We didn't even know he knew a woman.

Only those who attended this wedding would have believed it. The bride and groom invited us to an old granite pit, carved to the nines by a man named Bill Youngren. This stone bowl had been transformed into a sea of moats and a parade of Pleistocene monoliths. And there, smart Jimmy and sweet Jo Anne got married.

Although younger, Jo, was at the end of her oocytes, if you get my meaning. They tried to make a smart baby for two years, but it didn't take. So they did what many wonderful couples do in a similar situation. They purchased a high quality black dog. They loved Blackie like a child—a reasonable thing to do, if you ask me, though it's not quite the same as having a baby. Still, they pampered him even beyond what his pedigree—a Shiba Inu—demanded. All seemed content.

Then, when everyone was looking the other way, including Aunt Jo Anne, she became pregnant. It was the wonder of the world, for them at least. Jimmy, so smart that he'd missed the first wave of girls, and now so content with Jo Anne and Blackie, was going to be a father at fifty!

I don't remember when Jo Anne got sick, but it was bad from the start. The baby grew inside of her only a half step faster than the cancer, just fast enough to escape her mother's womb alive. Jo Anne lived long enough to see Larissa take a few steps, to hear her call Smart Jimmy "Daddy." And I believe that was long enough for her, though she would have stayed longer if given the choice.

She died on the first day of winter, and people talked about tragedy and loss, but Plum insisted they were wrong. A gleam in her eyes the day before she died told him a different story. She was the happiest woman in the world, watching her child in Jimmy's arms—happy enough to go away.

At the funeral Larissa was handed around, and many called her the angel in Jimmy's life. Plum pointed out that actually we had it all wrong. Jo Anne was the angel. Larissa was her magic harp. And Jimmy the soul, set back on its course by their music.

I met Plum's eyes.

"So Jo Anne was the angel?"

He nodded.

"And the baby?"

"Her gift to Jimmy so that he could go on."

"O.K. I believe in angels."

And we continued to walk among the weathered headstones at Seasoncreek's cemetery, looking for relatives long dead.

17. Cloning Moses

Everything changed when modern science arose, and the world decided for a short time that all religion was bunk. Of course, that system crashed when The Name was discovered, but when science was the biggest show in town, order reigned over chaos and the divine was silent.

All sorts of incredible discoveries that threatened normal life everywhere were made in the twentieth century. Watson and Crick came across DNA—deoxyribonucleic acid, if you care—in nineteen hundred and fifty-one, but nothing practical came from their work for fifty years. Then suddenly, lab rats—the human kind—around the world started to make use of the double helix, and the cloning began.

In Scotland, a scientist cloned a sheep from some ewe-nipple cells. In Prague, biochemists cloned a pancreas to make super-insulin. Rows of pancrei, one cloned from another, providing insulin for diabetics worldwide.

"No people, just pancrei!" Plum thought this was funny.

And when cloners started in on fetal brains, the sky was no limit.

"Boy, doesn't this cloning business seem a bit strange to you?" Plum asked me as we mulled over the latest clone-related-biotechnical-advance in the Tuesday New York Times science section. For me, the jury was still out. I didn't have a clear clone-position. But an argument with Plum was certainly brewing, so I had to think one up quickly.

"I suppose it is strange, Plum, but there's nothing really ever 'normal' about science. I don't care what Kuhn says. Grandpa once told me he felt strange about eating mold to get over pneumonia, but that was penicillin. Still, I will confess that I find mass produced pancreases are a little fringe."

"I don't mean that, Boy."

Plum was disappointed in me. "Those things are new and odd, of course, and yes, anything new always seems abnormal. But what strikes me as strange—unbelievable, even—is that people aren't cloning what makes them happiest."

"What do you think we should be cloning, Plum?"

"Isn't it obvious?"

"No," I answered, legitimately lost now. "What should we clone, Plum?"

"Moses of course!"

Let me explain a thing or two about Moses. Moses was a dog—the greatest dog that two boys like Plum and me ever loved. He was the puppy of our childhood, licking our almost six year old faces when we first met because Plum's head got stuck in his baseball cap. He was our full-grown canine protector when bullies threatened us on the middle school playground. And Moses was the elderly gentleman dog who passed away after we had left for the bigger outer world—college for me, I'm still not exactly sure what for Plum. Moses had been an Airedale fixture for almost our entire lives, and as horrible as this might sound, we were much sadder when Moses died that when most of our older relatives met their maker.

So now that the world was hell bent on reduplicating itself, Plum decided that we should clone our second best friend. Twenty years after his death, we set about cloning Moses.

It wasn't easy convincing famous scientists to clone a dead pet. They weren't just cloning anyone or anything then, although that's changing now. Still, we found a way into a path-breaking lab—my M.D. helped—and before we could be escorted—kicked—out, Plum made such a commotion that Gunther Duberhagen, the head scientist himself, left his large, airy, and cluttered office.

"What is going on here," The bushy-browed scientist bellowed when he saw a gangly civilian body in his very private, high-tech government laboratory. "Who let you into my world? Do you have an invitation?"

"If you want to know what's going on," I replied, "it's riches for you, and a dog for a me. And if you must know, I came into your 'private laboratory' without an invitation because none are being passed out."

Duberhagen, a recent Nobel prize-winning plasma chemist (I think I forgot to mention that) was speechless—completely unaccustomed to being confronted by anyone. But since I'd raised the issue of riches, he let me continue.

We explained the pet cloning idea—how America was full of pet owners desperate to have their beloved dog or cat or hamster or turtle live forever. (Or at least as long as they did.) G. Duberhagen's lab could be the answer to their wishes. Sure, the cost would be high, but can you really put a price on the resurrection of your best friend? The potential market was enormous, and the combination of Duberhagen's scientific acumen and Plum's extraordinarily enterprising mind could make it happen. The ethical problems? Non-existent. The world may be skittish about cloning humans, but who could object to cloning Spot?

Moses of course served as our test case. We extracted his DNA from some hairball forever impregnated into a favorite blanket he napped on. Duberhagen worked his magic, otherwise known as science, and twelve or thirteen weeks later he handed us a puppy. He was the absolute likeness of Moses, our dog from nearly three decades before. We marveled at the advance of modern science. Finally, a practical application! And that puppy took to us just as he had when we were six years old. We were young again.

The Idea Man

When Duberhagen saw the look on our faces, he knew we had a winner. Riches became fact. Once news of Moses hit, orders for pets long gone poured into Gunther's lab. And he took them all.

First he cloned the dog that played Lassie on the TV show in the 1950s, and the show resumed production six months later. Since millions were dying to get their pets back, the only real challenge was time.

Once supply met demand, society became much more tranquil. It was the greatest thing to happen in years, better than electricity, rock candy or the decentralized state. And yet, like most wonderful inventions and discoveries, our pet cloning took some curious turns before it was forced to make room for the next wonderful invention.

Within five years we felt our mission was complete, as most of the people of the world had their childhood pets back. What more could they want? Nothing, we thought. Wrong! Our idea had set scientists off on cloning almost all of the greater mammals—rhinos, elephants, kudu, giraffe, otters, lions, panda bears, and lemmings. As the science became more advanced and finely tuned, new cloning ideas began to take shape in the minds of men who had never owned a bunny or pony or any other gentle creature. These men had monsters in mind—the monsters of mankind.

A group in Cairo had been working secretly for years in parallel with Duberhagen's laboratory, but had achieved much less than our man. Embittered by this failure, a rogue element within their midst secretly began to use Gunther's methods for their own ends.

And here you need to know that even before the science of cloning was a remote reality, governments around the world had signed a Homo Sapiens No Clone

106

Pact. The reasoning, I suppose, was that having several copies of person running around could be confusing. Cloned criminals would be a menace—"How do you know it was this me that robbed your bank?"—and cloned Hare Krishnas . . . well, you get the idea. Whatever the reasons, world governments completely banned human cloning.

But good ideas find a way of meeting bad ends. Thanks to Gunther's hard work and Plum's good thinking, the technology had become so streamlined that less intelligent and well-meaning people entered the cloning game—some renegades from that Cairo contingent. Organized by a young and enterprising scientist-economist named Kareem Abdel-Motaal, the Egyptians began work on cloning the most renowned leader from their country's past.

Ramses the Enslaver.

What had therefore started out innocently with Moses was now about to reproduce the Pharaoh!

When news broke that Egypt had sponsored such a reckless experiment, the world was outraged—Jews worldwide were nervous and irate! And what to do with this baby Pharaoh? He was a person, after all—a very cute person, in fact. So despite such past activities as enslaving the Hebrew people and building monuments from their sweat to demanding Sun Gods, human rights groups argued that you can't simply condemn a clone, and especially one that was just a baby and hadn't caused any trouble. Yet.

The newly-formed International Committee for the Prevention of Human Cloning (ICPHC) shut down Motaal's lab ASAHP (as soon as humanly possible) but the damage had been done. The world was doing its best to control technology, but it never had before, and couldn't seem to now.

"You can't chain ideas," Plum said. "You really shouldn't bother trying to contain them. It just never works."

Plum was right, but it still bothered me.

Since people feared that if the Pharaoh grew up in Egypt history would repeat itself, the United Nations and the ICPHC decided to raise him in as neutral and apolitical an environment as possible. The Middle East was obviously out, and Europe's history of war and carnage meant no one wanted to let him teethe there either. (Even Switzerland was too political.) So the world settled on Bermuda. No Bermudan was on record as seeking world domination, so growing up there wouldn't be much of a concern. A Caribbean Pharaoh, even a Rasta prince, would have been manageable, if it had only stopped there.

The Pharaoh cloning set off a domino effect, as past political leaders and religious figures from the great dynasties were turned out by one nationalist/zealot after another in every corner of the world. Soon, little potential troublemakers began to sprout up everywhere. The Chinese—probably against even their own better judgment—cloned a baby Genghis Khan from ashes in his Great Highness's burial temple in Mongolia. An infant Attaturk hatched in Turkey, and a baby Mahatma Gandhi surfaced in New Delhi, courtesy of cells taken from one of his sacred sarongs (at least he was non-violent). Vladomir Illiovich Lenin rose up from his bony remains in Red Square, and by the time the world had managed to end human cloning entirely, the nursery included a baby Mussolini, Theodore Roosevelt, Joan of Arc, Martin Luther King III, Rasputin, Napoleon, and Arthur of Camelot. In an ICPHC-sponsored day care center on the beautiful island of Bermuda, not far from perfect white sandy beaches and crystal blue water, this precocious bunch of kids all turned out to be sweet children in the end. Supplied with a Bermudan nanny, a daily nap, and a cookie break, and absolutely, positively, no exposure to world politics, they were more than happy to cohabitate in that Caribbean sandbox. Pharaoh, Genghis, Vlady, Atta, Mahatma, Benny, Teddy, Joanie, Marty, Rasputin and Art were happy kids. Of course they all picked on Gandhi, but some things can't be helped.

As for their teenage years, I'd rather not get into that. (Joanie was very popular, but really didn't want to be.) They became a willful bunch but that's adolescence and another story for another day.

In the end, though, these youngsters never really caused too much trouble. The world survived, and Plum and I were devoted to our cloned Moses, the greatest dog ever returned to this world. Duberhagen? He retired to a very rich and quiet life of cloning giant tomatoes and sunflowers. And to the best of my knowledge, the world's scientists still avoid re-creating mankind, and especially its monsters. I think everyone is relieved.

18. That

There is a moment in a person's life when everything changes. It's that moment you think about forever, that moment that marks every day that you take a breath, say a prayer, or eat a meal. That is the moment when your life pivots around itself.

I went to my office late one night, maybe around one a.m. Still living the strange hours and nine-day weeks that Plum and I had agreed on years before, I did wear a watch. I often went to the office that late; it was a good time to think about life when no one else was around: family, patients, Ms. Pumpkin, or even Plum. I also liked my office more, now that I had spent ten or fifteen years there. I was more comfortable, if not more of a physician. Plum's oriental rug still adorned the floor, its exotic patterns trod thoroughly by me, and those who came to their town doctor for advice, medical or otherwise. That had become my role, a listener and advice giver, and it wasn't bad, really. Some doctors from my generation became pill pushers; others became butchers—that's the surgeon's lot usually, notwithstanding the excellent carving preformed by Quinlin, Reed, and the Evans brothers. The rest settled in someplace along a continuum between healer-expert and diagnostician-quack. I was happy to hear a patient out, and then suggest things that were unlikely to cause them any more pain than the world already distributes in ample measure. The townsfolk trusted me, and there's no greater compliment that a doctor can get. I'm certain that I didn't deserve their trust, but I appreciated it more than they knew.

When I turned the handle of my office door that night, my desk lamp was sending out a few rays of "there's-already-someone-in-here" light. It was Plum, sitting with his head in his hands.

"What are you doing here so late?" I asked. I wasn't bothered that Plum was at my desk. "Your best friend is the person you never mind seeing," he once told me.

"I'm in pain, Boy, and I can't shake it. I've been thinking about that."

"What?"

"That, Boy, that!"

"But what, Plum? What are you thinking about?"

"No, not what, that is what I'm thinking about. They're two totally different creatures, what and that, and that is making me sad."

Granted, Plum was often tricky to figure out. Sometimes I let his confusions go, and other times I'd probe for inner meaning, but it really didn't matter which tack I took. He was either in a talking mood or he wasn't. That night I had to wait hours for him to open up. I was too mixed up between that and what to ask a sensible question, so we just sat silently. Plum, lost in that moment that was troubling him so deeply. Me, just lost, but comfortable in the lounging chair with my feet up. Then he spoke.

"Do you remember your first love? Do you remember how your stomach felt when you first saw her? You get one moment like that in your life, if you're lucky. It's dew on daisies, desert water, double rainbows and chocolate waterfalls all combined. It's love. Every other waking moment is actually spent daydreaming that that dream might come true."

"Plum what's wrong? What's happened?"

"Every moment is connected, Boy. Each depends on the next. One rift, and it all falls apart. Life is a giant sphere of time revolving around itself. But all the moments aren't equal. One shines like a star. Everyone has that moment somewhere, though few people see it. Mine came and went, and I'm afraid that at that moment I let her slip away forever. I blew it."

This was the first time I had ever heard Plum talk about love. Despite all those years together, it had been absent from our dialogue. But then his mind was different— romantic in every way, yet never dreaming for himself. It occurred to me that since often love is just for yourself, he had never been selfish enough to be in love.

"Boy, I've been dreaming about a girl for as long as I can remember. You've met her many times at night, when I'm sleeping. You're actually old friends, though awake you've never met."

Plum was strange that night, but even stranger were the feelings I began to have, as Plum told me about his dream love, and I began to remember her.

"The three of us were inseparable as kids, Boy. The best of friends . . . "

"She had red hair!" I interrupted. "Didn't she Plum? Red and wild with freckles all over her!" Her image suddenly poured into my mind.

"And skinny, grinning toothless with a button nose," Plum added, "with legs like a colt."

"Faster than either of us, right?"

"Right, too fast to catch unless she let me. I knew you knew her. And when we got older, most of the freckles faded, and her skin became soft like rose petals."

I could feel it in his voice.

"Her beauty crept up on us and she often smiled at us because we were almost men, but definitely still boys. She was never far away. She laughed at our waking follies—the Monks, Walt at North Camp, Wolfgang, and Duberhagen. She waited up every night for our stories. When we didn't go to bed, she missed us terribly."

"When did you fall in love with her Plum?" I was remembering more about his dream girl every second.

"From the second I saw her, of course, though my childhood dreams weren't so intense. A child's love is different."

"But why are you so sad, Plum? What happened to her?" The way he spoke about her puzzled me. Where could a dream girl go, after all? They were his dreams.

"It's the funniest thing. For thirty years she was there every night, wandering my dreams with me. No one satisfied me like her. I was so happy that my conscious self started to wonder what was going on at night. So the conscious started to bother the unconscious, waking me up when I didn't want to. 'Tell her to wake up with us,' my mind said to my dreams, 'so the day is as good as the night.' Sensing the idea was a bad one, for years my unconscious just ignored the conscious. But as Freud and all the rest of the headshrinkers say, you can't just let the unconscious have its way all of the time. I didn't know what to do. I think now that I just didn't want to share her with the rest of the world.

"But things have a way of happening, even if you don't want them to. The constant badgering from my conscious mind forced me to reconsider. It was worst during afternoon naps, just when I was falling asleep—that moment when you're awake, and your leg twitches. At that moment, when the conscious awake world is blurring into the unconscious dream world, that's when the conscious laid on the pressure the thickest. 'Bring her out! Introduce us! Let's see this girl.' He wouldn't let up, and I would wake up. I wasn't getting any rest at all. Finally I promised that I would ask her to wake up with me.

"That next night I slept very, very deeply. My dream girl and I went to a place that seemed like Khazakstan, and in front of a purple mosque I popped the question. 'Will you wake up with me?'

"She smiled and turned away. Her red hair flowed over her shoulders, and her flowery blue sundress was dotted with daisies and marigolds.

'I can't,' she said.

'Why?' I said. 'You know that I love you.'

"People poured out around us from their midday prayers. 'I know you do,' she said, gently. 'But you won't like what will become of me if we wake up together.'

"I was hurt and confused by this. 'I'll love you as much as I do while we're asleep, I swear it!'

'We'll never survive the day.'

'What do you mean? How could that be? We love each other don't we?'

'Yes, Plum, I love you. But when you see your dreams up too close, they tend to fly away.'

"If I had only listened to her then. Months passed. Each night, I asked her again and again to wake up with me. Each night, I asked and she smiled but refused, giving the same reason as before. Each morning I would wake up without her. My conscious self was getting angry. Then one night, after I asked her, she smiled, but said something new.

'Plum, 'I'm going away. But don't be afraid. Boy will keep you company in your dreams, just as he does when you're awake. And I promise I'll return someday.'

"I was devastated. 'You can't go—I mean I don't want you to go. I don't understand.'

'People don't need to understand their foolish dreams. Just be patient. I'll be back someday.'

"And she vanished. At first, I just missed her. But as one dream followed another without her, I became desperate. At night I tried to search all of my past dreams, but she was nowhere to be found. Then I made that mistake that I'll regret forever. I began to search for her while I was awake.

"I told my conscious self all about her—what she loved and what she hated, where she liked to travel, and to rest. We started a waking quest to find her.

"I went to all the real places that I had always dreamed of, unconsciously visited with her time and again. Just as I was about to give up hope, I found myself standing in front of a majestic purple mosque in Khazakstan. Then unbelievably, if only I could have convinced myself not to believe it, I looked up and there she was, standing with her back to me— wearing the flowery blue dress dotted with daisies and marigolds, her long red hair flowing as it always did over her shoulders. I ran up behind her and put my arms around her, but when she turned around there were tears in her eyes.

'Why are you crying? Now we can be together day and night.'

'Because now I have to fly away.'

"A surge of people poured out of the mosque and enveloped us. I turned my head for a split second, and when I turned back around, she was gone! A white dove flew up into the air, circled the crowd once, and disappeared into the distance."

"What happened, Plum?"

"She flew away. Dreams do that, when you see them up too close. That's the last time I ever saw my dream girl, anywhere. Now I follow doves in my dreams. That was the moment my life pivoted around itself. That was my moment."

I noticed that the sun had begun to rise outside of my office window. No dreams for either of us tonight. Neither of us spoke for a long time. Plum broke the silence.

"Boy, do you know what love really is?"

I answered him honestly.

"No Plum, I don't."

19. Zig-the-Zag

"I miss the old days Plum."

"I know, Boy, but really there's nothing to miss. They're right there behind us all the time."

"That's my point, Plum. Those days are behind us—the best days of our life."

"I guess you haven't visited the past lately. Maybe it's time for a trip back, or forward, or however you prefer to think about things."

"What are you talking about?"

"I'm talking about paying our younger selves a visit."

"Time travel? Are you mad!" I laughed, leaning forward on my elbows, planted firmly on the oak desk between us.

"This is Seasoncreek, not some science fiction novel. And besides, where's the time machine or spaceship?"

Plum looked up from the book that he was reading—I think it was Milton's *Paradise Lost*—and with raised eyebrows, flared nostrils, and a big smile, he put me in my place.

"You're right, Boy. We don't have a spaceship or a time machine. Those other contraptions don't really work anyway. I don't care what Asimov says. But we do have something infinitely more practical for the trip. Our minds. One's brain is the ticket back, the mind will be our time machine."

"You've lost me."

"All right, Boy, let's go!" he said getting up to his feet. "You're right, it's a good idea. Let's go to the old days."

"Wait a minute, old buddy, is this some kind of joke?"

Had Plum finally gone completely insane once and for all, or was I was playing the fool again? I wouldn't have minded much, since he was my closest friend.

"Come with me," Plum said.

"But where?"

"Back to us, to what we once were!"

"When?"

"Before now and after then. It's time to Zig-the-Zag," Plum said, and closed his eyes. I did the same. I felt my temples pound as I tried to sort out Plum's crazy proposition. Zig-the-Zag? Going back when? After then?

"Plum, I am afraid I just don't under—"

I opened my eyes. Sitting in front of me was Larry Plum, reading a Marvel comic, five years old again. He looked up and met my bug-eyed stare.

"You see Boy, yesterday is only a Zig away."

I was three feet six inches tall!

"Plum!" My voice squeaked, "How, I mean what, I mean where are we?"

Plum smiled through the gap of his baby front teeth.

"Wrong three times! It's when, my friend. The correct question is when are we? We're boys again! We're five— that's when. We're zigging-the-zag together!"

There it was again. Zigging-the-zag.

"P-P-Plum," I stammered, trying hard to reacclimatize to my pint-sized-self, "can you take a minute to explain what's happened!"

"You mean when—" he started to correct me again, but I wouldn't have it.

"Yeah, whenever! What, when, how! Just do me a big favor and explain this! Please!"

I was upset, flummoxed, and disoriented, as you could tell from the tone of my voice if this wasn't a book. Plum took pity on me and explained.

"OK Boy, here's how it goes. Time isn't just a minute or a day or a second or a year."

"It's not?"

"Well it is, all of that and more. Time is a state of mind. The way I learned it—"

"From who?"

"That's not important right now. The way I learned it is that time is a zaggety line that runs through space, shifting unpredictably, ridable like a wave. More simply put, time is a zag in space, and to travel through time you—"

"Zig-the-Zag!"

"Exactly, Boy! Zigging-the-Zag is what brought us back. Back to five years old today, lord knows when to tomorrow!"

"But I don't understand how you did it, Plum. How did you get us back to our childhood?"

"I just opened my mind and let it take us where it wanted to go."

"That's all?"

"Yes, Boy. You just need to give your mind some time and space to wander. It will take you wherever and whenever you want to go, sometimes to places you don't even remember you've been."

Whatever his method, the truth was we were five again, and the old days that I had been missing were right in front of me. I'm not going to tell you about that wonderful week we spent as five-year-olds again back in Seasoncreek. What happened isn't really that important. The fact that it happened at all is what really matters most.

"Plum thank you for bringing me here. I think this was the something I needed—to be a boy again, even just for a few days."

"My pleasure Boy, only realize that it wasn't just me. Your mind did half of the wandering. Otherwise, I would have made this trip alone. Where should we go next?"

"I hadn't really thought of going anywhere except back to the present," I said with some hesitation, not really knowing what to call middle age in Seasoncreek anymore.

"That's OK, Boy, you can call that the present if you want. It doesn't have a better name."

"Where would you like to go Plum?"

"Well, Boy, I am curious about a certain time, only—" Plum scratched his head.

"What Plum? Only what?"

"Tell you what, Boy. Let's let our minds wander together, and see where they take us."

I closed my eyes and opened my mind while he did the same, and off we went, to Zig-the-Zag once more.

When I opened my eyes I was alone on a grassy plain. The hot sun baked my back, and flies were buzzing all around me.

"Plum, where are you?" I grunted, my voice sounding very deep and hoarse. I must have picked up a bug on our way.

"Turn around, I'm right behind you having a bite to eat."

My legs felt extremely heavy as I got up and turned around to see my friend.

"Darn these flies," I thought, "they're all over me. But I don't remember ever living near a meadow like this before."

Standing behind me was a horribly tall giraffe (is there any other kind?), pulling leaves from the top of a sycafuss tree with his two-foot-long tongue.

"My God, what's going on! What is this place? When is this place," I whispered, not expecting any reply. "And what is this beast doing here!"

"Beast, indeed! I'm offended! You had better take a good look at yourself!"

The giraffe then lowered his neck eight feet to make eye contact with me. I closed my eyes for a minute, opened them again, and looked myself over.

"My God, I'm a rhinoceros!"

My tree trunk legs felt a bit unsteady, so I settled to the ground with a crash, like the two-ton monster I was.

"Are you OK?" the giraffe asked. "You'd better be careful sitting down fast like that. You could cause an earthquake!"

He laughed, with a high-pitched giraffe-like whinny.

So this was how it was before we were boys. We were big game on the Serengeti, grazing the African plains. And what an incredible life it was! As a rhinoceros, life was particularly easy. I had no predators at all. Sure, some of the Neanderthals had spears, but come on! I had a horn, ran forty miles per hour, and weighed well over two thousand pounds. Hunter-gatherers were no match for the likes of me. So I just ate all day long. What a life!

The Idea Man

Giraffes, though, had lions to contend with. The big cats were usually happy with a kudu or a springbok, but every once in a while, one of them craved a longer leg, and the giraffe was off and running.

One day he was horsing around at a waterhole when two lionesses caught wind of him. (He really didn't smell all that good, frankly. You've been to the zoo.) The usual big-clumsy-cats chasing graceful-giraffe hunt ensued. I was napping in a dust pit when they came tearing by me the first time, so I paid the three of them little mind. On their second pass, though, one of those lionesses decided to have a little fun with the Rhino, and laid a claw across my rear end. That got my attention, so when I saw them closing in on that poor giraffe I stood up out of my pseudo-slumber and threw a shivering hip check into the alpha-cat. Believe me, when a rhino lays a hip into a lioness, I don't care how big she is, she feels it. That was the end of the day's hunt. She must have seen stars for a week, and the giraffe got away.

Later that night I had an unexpected visitor. I was out grazing again—that's all I did, really, graze and sleep—when the giraffe came trotting up to me.

"Rhinoceros! I want to thank you for saving my life today. I was in over my head." This was something hard to believe about someone seventeen feet tall!

"Don't mention it," I grunted, and continued my meal.

"No, you don't understand, Rhino. My name is Larry Plum, and I owe you one!"

"Fine, then. And you can call me Boy."

This was how we first really met!

A few weeks passed, and the fall was coming—not that it made much difference at that latitude. It was never any cooler than eighty degrees during the day—kind of like Honolulu. I hadn't seen Larry Plum the Giraffe, or much of anyone else for some time. Even as a rhino, I was a bit of a loner. The previous spring, I had left my family in search of my own family and fortune. But in a year, I hadn't met anyone. The hyenas laughed at me because I so wide. The lions were afraid of my temper. And the leopards and hippos had no time for conversation. Elitists! So I was feeling pretty lonely out on the range. Then things changed.

I was napping one afternoon in the shade of a Joshua tree when I felt a hooved nudge on my backside. "Wake up, Boy, if you don't mind."

"What is it?" I grumbled, not bothering to open my eyes, since nothing out there could eat me. "I'm asleep!"

I felt another kick, this time firmer and with more meaning.

"Wake up! There's someone here I want you to meet."

"This better be good, I need my beauty rest—"

"And badly, to be sure," said Plum the giraffe, "and this is very good."

I opened my large dusty eyes, shaking my three hundred pound head to clear them. Standing there with Plum was a vision—the most scrumptious woman I'd ever seen. Strong square jaw, tight eight hundred pound tuckus! And ohhhh what a horn! My heart stirred. She blushed.

"Rhino, this is—" he began.

"Boy, my name is Boy," I stammered, staring into her enormous round hazel eyes. She winked.

"Well, Boy, please meet Buttercup. She's new in town and—"

"It's a pleasure to meet you, Buttercup. Allow me to show you around the plain."

"I'd love to!" And it was love at first sight.

As you know, or at least can well imagine, rhinosori mate for life—two horns become one, so to speak. Buttercup and I were made for one another, and Plum had introduced us. When she delivered our first son, we named him Lawrence, and insisted that Plum be his godfather. And what a wonderful and tall giraffe-godfather he was.

This was the beginning of our great friendship, one that lasted far longer than a simple minded rhinoceros like myself could have ever imagined. But as Plum said then, and now—

"Like all truly great friendships it will last forever—and certainly more than a lifetime."

And so it has.

20. Lost Forever

"Why do the years pass so quickly as we get older? Why do the seasons speed by?" I asked Plum. We now seemed to be racing through life—though I'm happy to admit mine had been a good one.

"I hadn't noticed, Boy. Are things passing by quickly these days?"

"Yes! Jesus, Plum, we're aging fast! We're fifty!"

"How old?" He seemed surprised. "That can't be right, Boy, we're not fifty. What year is this?"

Was Plum serious? He was, so I told him what year it was—and also the date of our birth, just in case that had also slipped his mind. We did the math.

"Fifty!" Plum muttered to himself.

"You know, Plum, this is the kind of thing that people tend to keep track of. How old did you think we were?"

"I don't know. In our late thirties, or maybe our forties. What does it matter anyway?"

"I guess it doesn't matter, I just noticed how fast it's all going. We're half dead!"

"And half alive!" Plum smiled.

Which half, I wondered.

"So Plum, how did you lose ten or fifteen years along the way? I was genuinely curious. How could he let his mind wander so far that he had no memories for more than a decade?

"I suppose I've just had a lot on my mind, Boy. That's all."

"Fifteen years, Plum! What could possibly have occupied you like that?"

"The old wound, Boy. That's what has occupied me."

Only one quest could have cost him a decade of thought. Nothing else meant as much to him—except perhaps our friendship.

"Your middle name?"

Plum nodded.

"Any leads?"

He shook his head no.

"Boy, I'm afraid that it's lost forever."

"Plum, cheer up. We'll find it. Don't worry. Nothing's lost forever—nothing important, anyhow."

"Oh but Boy, you're wrong. Very important things have been lost forever. People just don't talk about them—it's too painful. My middle name just might be one of those things."

I was curious about what Plum meant by lost forever.

"Lost forever," he continued, "means lost and never coming back."

He was getting a little emotional, so he shifted to talking about the four most important things that were *lost forever.* Who would have known about them except Plum?

"In 1590, the most important lost forever play was, well—lost," Plum began.

"Never heard of it," I said.

"Exactly my point, Boy! But you would have heard of it, you and all the world, if only Shakespeare could have held his liquor."

"Who?" I was hoping I hadn't heard Plum correctly.

"Shakespeare! He wrote a perfect play about a pair of young lovers torn apart by their vain and proud families. It was a tragedy," Plum shook his head sadly, and wiped a tear from his eye.

"Plum, everyone knows Romeo and Juli—"

"Don't patronize me, Boy! I'm not talking about Romeo and Juliet! I'm talking about the other play, the lost forever play. The one that was better than Romeo and Juliet. The one he lost when he passed out in the alley behind the Governor's Pub after a heavy night of wine and cheese with the ladies if you know what I mean. Boozing! They say that Shakespeare himself said that this lost forever play was his opus, and he had to settle for Romeo and Juliet as a cheap knockoff years later. It broke the man."

"What was it called Plum? The lost play I mean?"

"He never told a soul," Plum stared off distantly into space.

Many minutes later, I broached the subject again.

"Ok Plum, what else was lost forever? You said there were four things."

Plum fixed his gaze on me.

"There was the Heisenberg Certainty Principle. That was a horrible loss—not Shakespeare, perhaps, but nothing could have been worse for particle physicists."

"The Heisenberg what, Plum?"

"Certainty Principle. The Certainty Principle!"

"All right, pal, explain it to me."

As a doctor I was a scientist only in the loosest sense of the word.

The Idea Man

"Well you've heard of Heisenberg, of course. He became famous in the early 20th century for his Uncertainty Principle. Remember Taylor's physics class in high school!"

I nodded the way people do when they're pretending to remember something they're too embarrassed to admit they've forgotten.

"I thought so," Plum laughed. "You never studied."

"Never mind, Plum. Well, what is it, this Principle?"

"The Heisenberg Uncertainty Principle tells us that it is impossible to know the position and momentum of a particle at any instant in time. You can know one or the other. How fast, or where, but never both. That's it."

"In English, please."

"OK, Boy. The change in location of an electron multiplied by the change in its momentum is always greater than or equal to Plank's constant divided by four times Pi. It's the cornerstone of particle physics, man!"

How could Plum know this? Or actually, maybe I should ask, how could Plum not know this, since he seemed to know almost everything else!

"So what's the big deal, Plum? We have Heisenberg's principle. This is about what was *lost forever*, remember?"

Plum nodded. He knew something important that I didn't—yet.

"Two days before he announced his famous *Uncertainty Principle*, Heisenberg was struck by true scientific inspiration. Equations of the most incredible complexity flooded into his mind, explaining the inner workings of the sub-atomic universe. He had an epiphany and a pencil, but no real paper where he sat. So he did what any resourceful scientific genius would, and wrote notes on the toilet paper at hand. He sat there for hours (which did cause some problems), writing down the *Heisenberg Certainty Principle*, and answering in the process all of the questions that remained about our universe. When he finished, he was so proud of himself that he immediately went off to celebrate what he knew was sure to change the world forever.

But he forgot one thing. His notes! When he awoke the next morning, he had a horrible pain in his stomach—and it wasn't gas. Where were the notes? Without them, he couldn't remember the answers he had conceived. Then he remembered where they were, and when he wrote them. He leapt out of bed and raced for the bathroom, only to see his six-year old son emerge, a tragic *fluuuussssssshhhhh* reverberating in Heisenberg's perfect ears. The notes were gone, and so was the *Certainty Principle*. As a result, at almost the same moment that the great *Heisenberg Uncertainty Principle* was born, its superior half-brother was *lost forever*.

"Tough," I said.

"You bet," Plum said.

The other two great things that were lost forever are really too painful to speak of in detail. Apparently Leonardo da Vinci painted a companion piece for the Mona Lisa, but he left it outside in the rain. He never painted her again, so the world will never know what she was smiling about. (This makes me cringe because I'm an art junkie; maybe it doesn't bother you so much.)

Plum then told me that right after Sergeant Pepper's, the Beatles left an entire songbook of unrecorded masterpieces in the back of the Queen's Rolls Royce, after a particularly heavy night of private enjoyment. Though none of them remembered any of the details, they all knew something great was lost forever. The songbook was never recovered. They all blamed Yoko. I do too. It was the beginning of the end.

If some of the greatest things in history were lost forever, then why not Plum's middle name too? Plum had spent more than a decade considering this possibility, and I was beginning to think he might be right.

"Plum what if it's true, and it is lost forever."

"Then I'm *lost forever*."

It was a terrifying thought, that a best friend could be lost forever. So what did I do? I helped him to find it—or at least to conclude that there was some hope it wasn't lost forever.

"Plum, your middle name has just migrated into the deep recesses of your brain. Maybe you just need some help in bringing it out again. Like one of your crazy ideas."

"What are you saying, Boy?"

"That's exactly it, Plum! I'm saying that I'll say your middle name, and you'll remember it when I do."

"That's not half bad, Boy. A lot of things get *lost forever* in our brains, don't they? More than we think, I bet. Maybe it's in here after all!" Plum shouted, pointing at his oversized head. "Maybe it's on the tip of your tongue!"

I actually credit dreaming up the idea of saying Plum's *lost forever* middle name to my discovery of a dusty and ancient version of *Random House's 5000 Baby Names* in my parents' things. It was our primary source in the game that was to commence.

"Abdul," I said.

"No, too Muslim."

"Addison, Plum?"

"No that's a disease." That's true. Addison's disease: a failure of the adrenal cortex.

"Aidan?"

"Forget it!"

"Albert?"

"I like it, but no."

"Alfred?"

"You know that means Elf counselor in Celtic, Boy. That's not it, though."

"Amandeep – very popular in Punjabi."

"Somewhat unlikely in this lifetime, but maybe next time. Move on, please."

"Arthur? You remember King—"

"Yes, of course I remember King Arthur. But it's not my middle name."

"Augustus?"

"What is it with you and rulers' names, Boy? Move on to the B's. I don't think it starts with an A."

"OK. Baron, Barry, Bart, Basil, or Benito?" I shot them off at him rapid fire.

"What was that fourth one? Basil? Larry Basil Plum? Nope, not quite right."

"Bilbo," I asked.

"Too Middle Earth," replied Plum, but smiling. He was very fond of Tolkien.

"Brendon, Brian, Brice, Brock, or Bruno?"

"No, no, no, no, and no."

"Well that's pretty much all for the B's, Plum."

"It's a fairly weak group don't you think, Boy?" Plum said, emphasizing the B in my name.

We passed through the C's and D's without much promise—Caesar, Carlito, Cedric, Chadwick, Chandler, Clayton, Clifford, Clinton, Colin, Connor, Cornelius, Curt, or Cyrus, then Dakota, Damian, Darrell, Dayne, Delbert, Demetrius, Deon, Devin, Dewayne, Dexter, Diego, Dimitri, Dion, Dirk, Duncan or Dylan. They all sounded ridiculous when placed between Lawrence and Plum. Then came the E's.

"Go on Boy, let's hear what you've got."

"Edgar," I began.

"Too FBI," said Plum.

"Eduardo," I countered.

"Too Spanish."

"Elvis."

"I don't have the sideburns for it."

"Enrique?"

"Even more Spanish!"

"How about Ervin, it means 'sea friend' you know? Or Eugene?"

"Lawrence Eugene Plum sounds almost right. Eugene is good but something is slightly off. Nope, that's wrong too."

"Well then, Ezekiel, or it's not an E!"

"No Boy, not Ezekiel, or any other E. We'd better move on," Plum said, though he was still half admiring Eugene.

In the F's I was partial to Fabian, Faulkner, Felix, Franklyn, and Fritz. But the only F middle name Plum considered for more than a half second was Fletcher, which I thought was completely absurd. He then agreed and we contemplated G.

There are a lot of quality middle names that begin with G it turns out.

I began with Gabriel and Galen, two excellent names I thought. Gabriel means *devoted to God* and Galen means *calm healer*. Plum hated them both.

So I spat out Garth, Gerrit, Giancarlo, Giuseppe, Gordon, Graham, and Gregor. The only name he liked was Gregor, because he was turned into a giant bug in Kafka's best story. But none of the G names fit Larry Plum.

The H's were fun. Hakim, Hardeep (another Punjabi attempt), and Heathcliff caught my eye. These were of course wrong, but I suggested them anyway. Plum considered a series of Greek and Latin possibilities— Hector, Horace and Homer among them—before rejecting them all himself. We sailed through H, though, with hardly a halt or hesitation, and immediately inquired into the I's.

This exercise was stimulating. After encountering all the Hebrew names—Ira, Irving, Isaac, Isaiah, Ishaq, Ismael, and Israel—we decided Jews have a stranglehold on names beginning with the letter I. Unfortunately, none of them belonged to Plum.

J, K, L, M and N took weeks to explore. Neither Plum or I became really optimistic about finding his middle name, but as our work progressed, and we discovered what Plum's middle name wasn't, I saw the joy of the search return to his life, as he began to believe that what was lost, wasn't necessarily lost forever.

Between J and N, I had a few personal favorites that I would have given Plum if that was what this was about. But it wasn't—we were out to find what was lost, and unfortunately Jamaal, Jarvis, Jazeps, Jonah, Joshua, Kareem, Kendrick, Konrad, Lawrence (I really liked this, Lawrence Lawrence Plum), Leo, Leopold, Luigi, Luther, Mack, Malcolm, Mandeep, Marvin, Maximillian, Miles, Moses, Mustafa, Nicolo, Nigel, Noah or Norman were just wrong.

One 'O' had real promise. From the second I said it, Oscar became the front-runner.

We looked it up to see if it fit Plum in any way. Oscar was the divine spearman from Scandinavian folklore. Plum leapt up onto my desktop. He thrust out his chest and jutted his chin. Then he reached way back with his right arm, producing an imaginary javelin from thin air. For a brief moment, divine spearman he was. With his left hand, Plum pointed off into the distance—my office kitchen—at an imaginary griffin or manticore, and uttered a guttural grunt. He cocked his magic invisible spear way back, and with an enormous roar let it fly right for my refrigerator. It flew through the air like an imaginary lightning bolt, and slew the horrible beast! But this divine spearmanship threw poor Plum terribly off balance. Trying to right himself, he arched his back 170 degrees, threw both arms straight out, and lifted his left leg up—all in an attempt to save his Scandinavian scalp from a dramatic fall. Too late. Plum crashed to the floor on top of me and his other invisible spears. The journals and papers on my desk flew in every direction. A twelve-pound edition of Harrison's Internal Medicine clunked Plum on his head, and he was staggered. He looked up at me, a little bleary-eyed.

"Not Oscar the divine spearman," I said.

"Oh no," Plum answered.

"Pablo."

"No."

"Paolo."

"No."

"Pasquale."

"No."

"Pedro."

"No."

"Pele."

"No."

"Pierre."

"No."

"Preston."

"No—no more P's please," said Plum.

"Quentin?"

"No."

"Quincy."

"No."

"Quintus," I said, laughing.

"No, not Quintus, Boy. Try R and I'll stop you if I hear it!"

"Rafael, Ramon, Ravi, Raymond, Remi, Reuben, Rex (I heard Plum grumble), Roberto, Rocco, Roosevelt, Roscoe, Roy, Rudolph, Rufus—"

"Go on to S," Plum said, unimpressed by R.

Time and the S's passed without a breakthrough.

"T's please," Plum said, from behind a newspaper.

"Ok Plum. Tanner, Thaddeus, Theodore, Tim, Tomas, Travis, Trev—"

"Don't even try Trevor on me, Boy!" As we all know, Trevor means 'prudent' in Welsh, and Plum was anything but prudent.

We rapidly approached the end of the alphabet. Ulysses the journeyman was an obvious possibility, I thought, or Virgil (Plum loved the *Aeneid*), or Wyatt (like in the wild, wild west), or Xerxes, or Yuri or Yevgenyi (which was really nothing more than Eugene in Russian), or even Zed. Some of the names sparked his interest, but fit snuggly between Lawrence and Plum. He shook his head no to all.

But instead of a long face and dim eyes, he was smiling.

"Plum, why are you so darn happy? That's it, that's the end of it, the end of the alphabet. We've come up empty again. I'm sorry."

"Don't be. You've given me hope again. My middle name may very well be lost, but I've never been more certain that it's not *lost forever*."

"Why are you certain, Plum? I can't think of any other names that would fit you. It's just not in here," I said, pointing to my average sized head.

"That's okay, Boy. You've tried, and that's what matters. And that's what you reminded me of, even if you didn't remind me of my middle name itself. Looking for things in life is what matters, and finding them is just icing on the mashed potatoes, or gravy on the cake. I'm sure my middle name is on the tip of someone's tongue. I just don't know whose!"

We didn't find Plum's middle name, but we did recover the joy of the search. One day he would find his middle name—he would find himself—and no part of my best friend would ever be lost forever.

21. The Arthurian Paradox

One summer we went wandering in southern England near Flaxonberg, a place also known as Old Saxony. Plum and me, that is. My wife and my two teenagers were on Nantucket, escaping Seasoncreek and me for July, so I was free to do as I pleased. Things were slow at the office, so I just put up the 'Be Back Soon' sign, and left. Seasoncreek had become accustomed to this, and frankly, Pumpkin could take care of almost everything herself.

The mud season in Britain was over, and the sun painted the countryside fifteen hours a day. I highly recommend wandering there at that time of the year. Our schedule? Wake and walk until lunch, then nap and walk until supper. We spent the rest of our energy on philosophy—mostly Plum's—and beer.

Then I tripped face first over God knows what.

It shocked me how time had ravaged my epidermis. My tight elastic skin had become a thinner and looser covering that barely kept rainwater out, or my own blood in. My knees were torn, my elbows scraped, and my scalp was lacerated. I was a bloody mess.

"Plum, give me a hand."

"Just a second, old Boy, I'm onto something here."

The Idea Man

Looking up through the gentle stream of blood dripping from my scalp, I saw Plum inspecting the cause of my fall.

"What is it, Plum? A root? Cobblestone? Dead squirrel?"

"None of the three. You've stumbled right over history, Boy, and it was definitely worth the fall!"

"For you, maybe! You're not the one bleeding!"

Plum walked over to me, and examined my wounds.

"Oh you're not so bad. Nothing fractured, I'm sure, and certainly no worse than my forehead in Bug's observatory. And I'll give you credit for the find!"

He helped me to my feet, and then introduced me to my downfall.

"What is it?" I said, gazing at what looked like an upside-down metal T stuck in the ancient side road. I forgot all about my cuts and bruises.

"I don't know! It looks old!"

We brushed away the dirt where the road met the base of the thing, and uncovered a line of perfect ruby-red gems. "And valuable. It must be worth a fortune!" I pulled, but it wouldn't budge. Plum came over, and the two of us counted. "One, two, three!"

Out of the baked Anglican earth came a glimmering and perfect blade in the sunlight—an ancient sword! Even though we had pulled it from the ground with just a single try, for some reason I felt exhausted. It was as though I had wrestled Enkidu for two nights and a day! I collapsed in the grass beside the road, absorbing the British sun, while Plum held the blade up to his face, inspecting its runic inscription with his keen eyes.

"My god, Boy, do you have any idea what we've found?"

"What is it, Plum? What does it say?"

"It can't be—it can't be."

"What for God's sake? Whose sword was that, and why was it stuck in the road in the middle of nowhere?"

"This nowhere was clearly somewhere before now!"

"Where?"

"This is Arthur's sword," Plum whispered.

"What?"

"We're standing on Camelot. THIS IS EXCALIBUR!"

A short note to the British Academy of History, and the archaeological invasion began. They hired virtually every digger in Europe. I knew very little about formal archaeology, though Plum had a surprising depth of knowledge on the subject, courtesy perhaps of his adventures during my college and medical school years. Nevertheless, as the discoverers, we were given an honorary supervisory role over the site. We had no authority whatsoever, but we did have an excellent view of the site from a hilltop, and enjoyed fine meals and hot tea thrice daily. The situation was perfect for us. We didn't work a lick, and the Brits who greatly appreciated our find (even if we were 'two Yanks') showed us all of the amazing artifacts that Camelot had to offer. This was the biggest thing since Imhotep!

On Monday the archaeological team unearthed Sir Gawain's shield. Wednesday revealed Queen Gueneviere's earrings. On Thursday, the site produced a staff that they decided belonged to the wizard, Merlin. Then the crown jewel, even more important than Excalibur, the King's sword that emerged from the ground. The crew rolled in this perfect, polished marble surface into our tent. The world was awestruck. Arthur's dining room set had reappeared, and that night, Plum and I had our tea and biscuits at The Round Table!

Plum was giddy, but I felt differently. After weeks away from Seasoncreek, I was depressed.

"Boy what is it? You're not yourself."

"I know, but I just don't know why. This should be the shining moment of my lifetime. We've found Camelot for God's sake! We're the envy of the planet!" I said, drawing Excalibur from its sheath. (The British were nice enough to let us keep it in the tent.) "But I can't shake this funk. What am I doing, Plum? How did I get here?"

We sat across from one another in silence, as we did in my doctor's office back home. The early morning became night. Plum paced back and forth in our luxury-tent, Excalibur now in his right hand, considering my dilemma. Then he spoke.

"It's the Arthurian Paradox, Boy. That's what has you in its grips. You're not you, because you can't decide who to be—just like Arthur."

This was quite a way to break the silence.

"The Arthurian what, Plum?" I answered

I had no idea what he was talking about.

"Paradox, Boy, the Arthurian Paradox. It's what haunted Arthur when he was the King of England, and now it's haunting you."

I watched Plum rend the air with King Arthur's ancient weapon, then listened, as he began to explain my demon to me, to save me from my depression.

"Boy, did you know that when Arthur became king, when he drew the sword from the stone, he was just an eleven year old boy? A Boy King graced and cursed by his destiny. In an instant, he went from contented stable boy to king of all England. No time for puberty, or knighthood, or anything else in between. That would do a number on your psyche, if you let it.

"Now because he was a great young man, the supernatural leader of the medieval world, the knights of that round table rallied around him, and he easily conquered his empire. Arthur was supreme. Forget about Mordred—Arthur ruled in peace almost his entire life. The pagans were subdued and mellow, and none of his people wanted for anything—except him! His fate had given him a kingdom, but not a life. Arthur felt torn in two. So you see, being king was also a curse. Of course at the beginning, Merlin had served as a best friend and counselor, but Arthur still felt he was alone. King Arthur needed friends, and love.

"He famously found a friend. Sir Lancelot. They became as close as brothers, and he felt much better. But Lancelot wasn't enough. He needed love, too. 'A king must marry,' he said, and sought out a true love. Guinevere. She was beautiful and kind—the Queen of queens, the only woman on this earth for Arthur, the only woman on earth for Camelot. Arthur loved her, and made her his queen. Fate had seemingly honored the greatest king, the Boy King, King Arthur. But 'all things must be balanced,' Merlin warned, and that same fate 'must curse the King that it blessed.'

"Guinevere and Lancelot grew to love each other, and they betrayed Arthur. He then had to become their judge. It was his job, and his worst nightmare. And there is the paradox, Boy—the Arthurian Paradox. To be a man or a King? To love or to judge? To live or to discover?

"Arthur's choices tore at his soul. He loved Guinevere and Lancelot. Perhaps if he was not their king, and just a man, he could keep his love for them. But Arthur knew he was born to be king, to be 'the stuff of future memory,' and not a man, at least in this lifetime. So Arthur judged them, Guinevere and Lancelot. He remained King, and Camelot was saved—or the memory of Camelot, anyway. But he lost all he cared for in the bargain. Arthur faced his paradox—to be a man, or to be king, a man or a myth—and he passed his test. And now he lives inside of us all forever. But then he was alone.

"You see, Boy, we all come to a place in life where we have to make a choice."

Plum sheathed the sword and sat down quietly, looking to me for my answer. The Arthurian Paradox was before me, just as it is for every man and woman. Camelot had its claws in me, but Seasoncreek, my home, awaited my return. It missed me and I missed it. I was torn, but I smiled when I made my choice.

"Let's go home, Plum," I said, half-asking for his approval to leave the newfound magic of Camelot behind.

Plum smiled back.

"Good choice, Boy."

22. All Men Go Bald

We grew old, Plum and I—older anyway— For me, haircuts were scheduled much less frequently, and combing became an afterthought. Showering was simpler; shampoo expenses diminished.

"Plum, I'm going bald!" I said to him across the oak desk that like my medical practice had miraculously survived so many years of benign neglect. They had aged gracefully—but had I?

"I know, Boy, we all are," he replied, not even bothering to survey the all-too-exposed terrain of my cranium. "All men go bald. It's the best kept secret in the Western world."

"We don't all go bald, Plum! I can name at least twenty close acquaintances of ours that have their hair—"

"Impostors!" he cried. "All men go bald, period. Most somehow cover it up. It's an illusion, Boy—hair, smoke and mirrors."

"You haven't gone bald, Plum," I said, jealously admiring his thick and wavy brown hair.

"Not yet," he said pleasantly.

"So what you're suggesting, Master Plum, is that there is an ongoing conspiracy—"

"A hair cover-up."

"—to have everyone believe that some men go bald, while others have the good fortune of keeping their locks until the bitter end. Why?"

It was the only reasonable question I could come up with on the spot, though "How?" had also crossed my mind. "How?" wasn't a bad question, but "Why?" is always so much more compelling!

"Why?" Plum responded. "I believe it's because the hair runs out, though I've never read anything completely satisfactory on the subject. Something to do with follicle burnout, I think."

"No, Plum. Not 'Why don't we have any hair?' Why is there a cover up?"

"Oh, I'm sorry. OK. Yes, then, why is there a cover-up over something as meaningless as baldness? That is a good question. Let's make it a better one. Let's ask, if you don't mind, the question underneath all of this insanity. Why do people try to become something that they're really not? Now that's a question!"

Plum was excited now, and who was I to slow him down (even though I only wanted to know who was behind the baldness conspiracy)?

"The answer is fear, Boy—fear of rejection, fear of having one's real self judged. It's the fear of not being good enough, and the fear of being alone. Fear, fear, fear, fear, fear."

Five fears! That seemed like a lot.

"But Plum, how does becoming something different protect you from being rejected, or judged, or alone?"

"It doesn't! That's my point Boy! It's just a gimmick— smoke and mirrors, remember? But people who try to change who they are to escape being judged end up even more alone in the end. They're just—"

"Hairier," I replied.

Plum smiled from ear to ear.

"Yes, Boy, that's exactly right! Hairier, or thinner, or richer, or whatever else you can imagine people trying to become in order to escape who they are. But they're never less afraid or less alone."

"OK Plum, but where's the conspiracy in all of this? Can't people do what they want—replace their hair, get tattooed, augment their breasts, have a nipple pierced, or whatever else makes them feel good?"

"They can have a big-hairy-tattooed-pierced-third-nipple added if they want. That's not the point. People should do exactly what they want for themselves, every waking minute of every day. What they want is the key, though. They shouldn't feel like they need to change. Needs need to be personal. And there's the conspiracy. Telling people what to be!"

Now it was clearer what Plum was talking about. There wasn't anything inherently wrong lurking in the hair replacement center, or at the gym where the muscle-heads lived, or at the weight loss clubs where team dieting had recently become a craze. The conspiracy, the evil if you will, was being convinced by someone who didn't know you, who had never met you before, that you weren't good enough. According to the world, for instance, being bald always makes matters worse. But then Plum dropped the A-bomb.

"You know, Boy, Albert Einstein was bald!"

"Einstein?"

"Bald as a baby's butt! The government put that crazy uprush of white hair on him so we'd have an image to associate with E = mc2. And he bought it too! Einstein! Wasn't sure people would accept him for who he was, even with all his great ideas."

"You're kidding me. Special relativity Einstein? General relativity Einstein? Relativity Einstein? Is no one safe?"

"No one."

"Who else was bald?" I asked, still reeling from Albert.

"Obama."

"No!"

Plum nodded.

"Barack Obama? That can't be true. I've seen footage of him getting a hair cut. You're wrong there, Plum. Wrong, wrong, wrong."

"I'm sorry, Boy, but that was a phony film, or worked up pictures. No haircuts for Obama, just hairpiece adjustments. The political polls didn't work with a bald-headed Obama, as great as he was, so he took certain liberties."

"But why go to all the trouble?"

"Sarah Palin."

"Of course."

That was reason enough for anyone.

"Fine, Plum, I'll give you Obama, and I suppose Einstein. But that's it. No more of my heroes."

I looked at Plum as he began wagging his index finger at me, suggesting he had a final name up his sleeve—one last hair-replaced public icon. "Well, Plum, you might as well tell me, or else I'll be thinking about it all day. Who is it? Let me see . . ."

"Mahatma Gandhi," he said, before I could offer my own guess.

"But Plum, that's absurd! Gandhi *was* bald—absolutely and completely hairless."

"That's my point," he said, as if I should understand—
which of course I didn't.

"I thought the issue was bald men adding hair—hair
replacements," I said, entirely confused.

"No, Boy. The issue was being something you're
not. Gandhi actually had a beautiful head of hair when
he started leading the salt marches, and advocating
nonviolent disobedience. He was still twenty years away
from the standard receding-hairline-pattern-baldness
phenomenon. It was his barber's idea to shave him bald
for the peaceful revolution. It gave Gandhi a kind of neo-
Buddhist-at-one-with-the-world-touchy-feely-appearance
that the movement needed. And it worked, too. But the
point is, that Gandhi bought into it. India was a free state
in half the time that it would have taken had Gandhi kept
his hair."

"But they shot Gandhi."

"Well you can't have everything. A model for world
peace, with or without hair, will have to be enough."

23. Plum's Middle Name

"Mittleshmertz! It has to be mittleshmertz!" I said, hoping that Plum would take notice of me and snap out of his trance. He hadn't said a word in five hours. Where was he?

I continued.

"Mittleshmertz is the phantom pain that plagues the abdomen of 31% of women at mid-menstrual cycle—"

"Of course," Plum muttered.

"Ah, so you are here in the room with me after all, Professor Plum. I thought you might join me here sometime tonight. But how do you know about Mittlesh—"

"Of course that's where I lost it. We had better go back and pick it up, before it's really *lost forever*!"

It was the middle of the night.

"What are you talking about, Plum? What could be so important that we have to find it in the middle of the night?"

"My middle name, Boy!"

"What?"

"Remember the hole when we were eight? We may not have dug it up then, but I've been searching for it ever since!"

He was quite serious, staring me right in my good eye. I had thought we were just messing around digging the hole when we were kids, but I was clearly mistaken.

"Okay, when exactly did you lose your middle name, Plum?"

"Don't be obtuse, Boy. Sometime after my first name, and before my last, obviously."

A flash of that Plum brilliance was in his eyes.

"But if you mean exactly when, I'm afraid I'm not sure. Certainly before we met — I was small."

"But how could you lose your middle name?"

I thought this might be a good place to begin.

"An excellent question, my ever curious doctor," Plum snapped back. "How could I lose that middle name of mine? How? How? An excellent question!"

His brow furrowed itself fifteen times, his hands supporting that aging but powerful jaw, made all the stronger by the endless conversations that had consumed us for seven decades. Plum was deep in thought, muttering. Then —

"Yes! That's it! I remember how, when, where!"

He then leapt to his feet, and dashed out of my office through the front door.

It happened so quickly that I was still butt-affixed to my desk chair when Plum's head came peeking around the doorframe back into my office.

"Why are you still sitting there, good old Boy? Leg cramp? Aren't you coming?"

"Give me half a moment," I said, smiling, "but of course I'm coming."

Where, I had no idea, but it hardly mattered.

"So where is your middle name leading us?"

"My former middle name you mean."

"Your former middle name?"

"That's right, Boy. I have realized that a long time ago, I lost my middle name half way around the world in a game of chance to a man named Budd. Are you satisfied? And I had forgotten all about him! What a trickster—he must have made me forget!"

With that he clasped me by the shoulder, drew me to my feet, and ushered me out the front door in search of Budd, the possessor of Larry Plum's middle name.

Plum and I were now well into our seventies, but we were still spry, and that counts for something. The Seasoncreek folk still wondered at our eccentricities, just as they had when we were in high school sixty years before. Few had understood us then, and even fewer understood us now (most of the old-timers were dead). It hardly mattered. Plum and I weren't going to change. "If you change your life do it for your own reasons not someone else's!"—Plum's wisdom echoed always in my mind.

So the two of us dashed—slowly—out of my office. We stopped by the house for a few necessities. I kissed my wife good-bye (I've already told you I had one—a great woman) and told her we would be back before long. Odd, I know, but by now she was used to it. And off we went— two old friends in search of one middle name.

Some adventures lie just around the corner—others don't. This one lay halfway around the world, on the top of a hill in Thailand, more than a full day's journey north of Bangkok. But the distance didn't matter much. "Finding one's middle name always takes precedence over work," said Plum, putting things into perspective as usual. So we weren't really even tired when we arrived in that little town without a name twelve thousand miles from Seasoncreek, and three and a half days after we rushed out of my office.

"Well, this is it, Boy. And it's just like I remember."

Plum dropped his small bag on the ground. I just raised my eyebrows. "This" was nothing.

The town was a tiny huddling of houses built at a point where thick brush perpetually threatened to engulf the beautiful Thai people who lived there. The place was tropical to an extreme. One hundred and ninety inches of annual rainfall meant the grass and brush grew quickly. Built from thatch and other green grasses, the houses flanked an ancient cobblestone road that wound its way up the hill. We followed it. At the end of the road was a roughly hewn staircase, passing up through a magnificent archway that sparkled green wherever sunlight touched it. Two feet thick, thirteen feet high at its apex, and twenty feet across, that arch was made of jade!

Carved first by men and then by wind, the jade arch was covered with mysterious and religious images. Gods and specters, ghosts and deities intermingled, all sharing in the secrets of the world, frozen there forever.

"This is the Eighth Wonder of the World, Boy," Plum whispered in my ear. "Not many people know about it, though. That's good. It helps to keep the foot traffic down."

I nodded, and we passed through the jade arch, and on into a cavern, and complete darkness.

"It's all just like I remember," Plum said.

I could hear him, but I couldn't see a thing. Then, far ahead in the dark distance, a sliver of light escaped from a lantern. I started to get a little nervous, there in the dark, with just the bats and that bit of light. The floor and walls felt cool and slippery in the pitch-black cavern. I couldn't see anything, but then Plum had left me in the dark on so many of our adventures' details.

"Plum," I said, in a hollered-whisper, which echoed five times, "when you were last here, who was holding that lantern?"

"Shhhhhh!"

Plum was still moving ahead.

"No, I mean it! I want to know what we're in for. Or who we're in for. What are we really doing here?"

A mix of anxiety, fear, and curiosity had welled up inside of me—that, and an intense need to pee. I couldn't check my emotions any longer.

"Well?"

"All right, Boy, calm down! I was last here when I was four years old," Plum said very quietly. The light source was growing much brighter now—a large lantern in the hand of a man sitting cross-legged on an enormous jade pedestal. Soon we were smack dab in front of him.

The man's eyes gleamed in an eerie way that was so familiar, so absolutely familiar, as if I had looked at them my entire life. They were in fact Plum's eyes! Even though Plum was standing next to me. They were exactly the same!

The man was angelic, though to be honest, he seemed a bit devilish too. There's a fine line between the two, and as we moved even closer, I was afraid of exactly that line. But when I saw his face clearly, all of my fears melted away, replaced by wonder.

The man was enormously fat, and entirely hairless. His face was as smooth as a baby's, and that made him seem probably a couple of hundred years younger than he really was. Of course, I knew that Plum had met him seventy years before, and he was already old then. But his plumpness gave him a quality of perpetual, mystical youth, and his gleaming eyes were time itself.

"I recognize your face," the man said, focusing all of his attention on Plum. "Older, yes, but the same. It's been a while, hasn't it?"

"A long time, a very long time," Plum replied, his eyes hawk-sharp on the man. "Budd, your memory isn't as good as I would have guessed. I figured you were omniscient!"

"Well, give me a moment, young man. I've met quite a few people in my day. Let me think now, when did we meet?" With that, the bald-angelic-enormity lifted his jolly torso up off the platform with his hands, and re-crossed his legs beneath him, as a much thinner yogi might. He closed his eyes, folded his hands in his lap, and hummed a sonic boom. *"Ohmmmmmmm!"*

The sound penetrated the walls around us, the ceiling above, the earth below, the roots of trees, and our ears most of all. After what seemed an eternity— *"Ohmmmmmm, Ohmmmmmm, Ohmmmmmmmm!"*—the sound finally broke. My teeth were vibrating. Budd opened his eyes, and stared at Plum again. Then a huge and benignly peaceful smile spread from chunky earlobe to earlobe across his face.

"Lawrence Plum!" he declared. "That's right, isn't it? Your name is Lawrence Plum! You were quite a curious little boy when we last met. How long has it been, Mr. Plum?"

"Seventy-two years," Plum answered, smiling to match the rotund master's expression. "You haven't changed much, Budd, though you seem a bit wider-in-the-waistband than I remember!"

"Now be nice, Plum," he said, "Mine is a life of contemplation, after all. I'm no jogger. Surely I can be forgiven a pound or two. And what about you, Plum? Has your life been full of adventure, mystery, enlightenment, and friendships?" With the word "friendships," he turned his eyes on me, and I shook in my shoes. This man had a presence as large as his waist.

"Yes, in fact it has, Budd," Plum said, addressing the rotundity by his name again. "Meet my closest friend in this world. This is Boy. He's a doctor and a curious person just like me."

"It's good to meet you, Boy. If you are half as curious as your friend Plum was when I first met him, then you're four times more curious than ninety percent of the curious people I've met in my own curious lifetime, which I can say has been extraordinarily long. At any rate, it's a pleasure to make your acquaintance."

To my amazement, the ancient-fat-guru then shook my hand and laughed a deep jovial laugh while doing it, putting me at ease.

"And call me Budd. That's my first name, at least given the way you Westerners think about things."

"Why don't you tell Boy here the rest of your name? I think he might be interested in it!" Plum said.

Budd shot a penetrating glance at him, and I thought for a second that Plum would take a step back from the force of it. But he stood his ground.

"No, that would be entirely too boring for an educated man like Boy here. It's quite long, after all."

"Some would say too long," Plum added.

"Yes some might say that," continued Budd, "but it is not really of any importance to Boy here."

These two were having some kind of pointed contest, so I called them on it.

"I don't mean to intrude, but what exactly is going on between the two of you? It seems there's some personal baggage that dates back to when Plum was a boy, and you, Mr. Budd, were—"

"Thinner!" Plum said.

I didn't want to be in the middle of their battle, so I kept my mouth shut.

"Yes, it's true, Boy," Budd began again, "your friend Plum and I do go way back. But I'm not sure what he wants from me now."

"I'll tell you what I want! I want what you took from me when I was just a boy! I want my middle name back!"

"Is that it, Plum? You want your middle name back. Don't you think that's somewhat hypocritical, coming from someone who doesn't even use his first name! I'm afraid I cannot help you. You can't have it!"

"Why?'

Plum was getting desperate.

"You can't have it," Budd answered him calmly, "a deal is a deal!"

"Deal? What deal, Plum? What is Budd talking about? You told me that you lost your middle name!"

"Well," Plum began, with a little hesitation, "I know what I said, but it is a little more complicated than that."

"*Complicated?*"

"I did lose it—but lost it to him! Why don't you explain it to my friend, Budd. You tell Boy how you took my middle name many decades ago!"

I turned to the corpulent philosopher, waiting for his side of the story. He squirmed a bit on his pedestal beneath the gaze of two friends as close as brothers, who wanted to know why any man would have taken advantage of a four year old Larry Plum, snatching his middle name away. After a pause, Budd began the tale.

"As you gentlemen know, seventy-two years ago, give or take a day, a boy came to this country. An adventure was arranged—a hike in the hills with two experienced guides. Young Larry Plum was to walk in Chiang Mai, where he might get to see a wild boar, a waterfall, and maybe even a tiger if he was very lucky.

"Well, Larry Plum was a very lucky boy, as we know, and he saw all three of these magical things—a tiger chasing a wild boar underneath a waterfall, if you can believe it! Content that they had entertained this curious four year old, the guides lay down for their daily afternoon nap, to escape the midday Thai sun.

"The guides assumed that young Plum was doing the same thing, and they quickly fell into deep snoring sleep. But they were wrong. Young Plum had closed his eyes to trick his guides, adding an occasional cute little boy snore to convince them he was asleep. As soon as they were out, he jumped up and slipped away.

" Earlier that afternoon, Plum and his guides had passed a cave with a very mysterious green arch at its opening.

'What's in there?' Plum had asked. 'Let's go in there!'

"But the guides had pulled him away. 'No! That is a dark, and a dank, and a dangerous place, with an ogre in it who likes the taste of little American boys! You can't go in there!'

"But given his naturally curious nature, Plum of course did want to go into the cave. So when that was the first place his little legs ran. At its entrance, young Plum was nervous for a moment, because it was so dark inside. But he pushed ahead. Inside was the long path leading back to the bright and shimmering lantern in the hand of a well proportioned and handsome bald man sitting on a pedestal of jade. No ogre, just this dashing man sitting cross-legged, meditating on the meaning of life. 'Hello,' the small boy said in a squeaky small voice, awakening the stunningly charismatic man's trance, but not affecting the *Ohmmmmmmm* that buzzed on his lips.

'Hello again,' the boy said, this time climbing up onto the jade platform and tapping the man on his shoulder.

"The *Ohmmmmmmming* stopped, the man's eyes opened, and he smiled at the boy. 'How can I help you, little man?' the man said to the curious little person.

The Idea Man

'Are you an ogre? Who are you? What's your name? What are you doing? Where do you come from?'

'That's an awful lot of questions from someone so short. I am Buddha, the seeker and obtainer of wisdom in this world. I come from times and places no mortal has experienced. I am all-knowing!'

'But now you live in this cave napping and humming all day in the dark with your legs crossed—right?'

'Yes, that is basically right my little man. Is there anything else that you would like to know before I return to my meditations?'

'Yes there is, Mr. Budd,' the boy said leaving off part of my name as little people are prone to do. 'I'd like to know where all of the animals come from, especially the camels. And why the sky is blue, and the ocean is green. Why do stars only shine at night, and why does the moon stare at me? Why do birds fly, and why do snakes crawl? What are leeches for, and what does *take your time* mean? What came before space, and why do only humans talk?'

'Is that all?' the man asked.

'No, Plum said, 'I have one more question.'

'Yes, son.'

'What happens when a boy grows up?'

"He clearly had a lot of questions—even for a boy that age. And to be honest, I didn't have all of the answers yet, though I'm working on it. I explained to the boy that walking the path of wisdom depended on asking the right questions. But he said, 'I don't know what that means, Mr. Budd. How can you walk on wisdom?'

"It was then I realized that easy metaphors and philosophical-double-talk aren't worth their weight in air. What a lesson from a young boy! 'What's your name?' I asked him.

'Larry Plum, sir.'

'Young Larry—'

'Plum sir, call me Plum! My friends do.'

'OK, young Plum, all the answers to your questions are in the world around you—deep in holes and in gumball machines, around the corner, in freckled faces, over hilltops, and mostly in the secrets people don't tell. But sometimes they aren't so easy to recognize, even if they're right in front of your face, or if someone whispers them right into your ear. Only a special mind can unravel the mysteries of the Universe—a mind full of its own ideas. Only an Idea Man can unravel them!'

'Do you know an Idea Man?' said Plum, 'I want to meet one!'

"And I looked closely into young Plum's heart, and seeing that it was good, I smiled at his warmth of spirit.

"And that's when the deal went down!" interrupted Plum. "That's when Budd gave me his blessing, and sent me trotting off on my four year old way sans my middle name!"

I looked up at Buddha, and I looked at Plum.

"So what happened?" I asked. "What went on between you two? What was the deal?

"You have to understand, Boy. The story didn't end with a pat on the head and Plum trotting off. He wouldn't leave me alone! I had thinking to do, but my answers were too obscure and evasive for him, so every time I began my chants, attempting to pass once more into the ethereal plane of knowledge and wisdom, he would tap my shoulder, or jump onto my lap, or throw small pebbles at my bald head. I was getting desperate! I had a lot of work to do!"

The Idea Man

Budd sounded a little strung out just recalling Plum's persistence. And Plum was laughing quietly to himself at the memory.

"So I said to the boy at last, 'All right! What do I have to do, Master Plum to get you to go back to your guides and to leave me alone? What's will it take?'

'I want a mind like yours, big Budd!'

"I was shocked. A four-year old demanding enlightenment! 'What if I just tell you where camels come from? Will that do?'

'No!'

'OK. How about the origins of the sky and the water? That's a big one, Plum! Almost nobody else knows how they began. You'll definitely be the only kid who—"

'No! Just the open mind if you please. I can figure out the rest on my own. I want to be an Idea Man, like you!'

"The boy's eyes sparkled. I had to think about this. I had never known a mortal Idea Man before, though I had heard rumors of a few. I wrestled long and hard with the idea. And in the end, I decided 'What the heck. You can always trust the mind of an innocent,' so I spoke to him. 'OK young Plum. If I'm going to do this for you, what will you give me in return? Open minds don't come for free, you know!'

"I said this, still half-hoping to discourage the little troublemaker and send him on his way. He emptied his pockets of string and rocks and a yo-yo, but I told him these weren't enough for an open mind. He jumped down from the pedestal, and took a few dejected steps toward the exit of my cave, his head hanging on his chest. I felt badly for the tyke, but it was a pretty good first lesson for someone so young. You can't have everything in life. And besides, since the work of enlightenment is no easy day job, I was saving him a mighty hassle. Then, just when I thought he was gone, and I was proceeding back into my standard trance, Plum came bounding back, and leapt back up onto my lap.

'I've got it, Mr. Budd! I'll trade you my middle name for an open mind! It's worth as much as anything that I've got! Take it or leave it!'

"This I had to admit it was an inspired idea from such a young person. He was probably destined to be an Idea Man with or without my help anyway. 'That seems fair, Plum. In exchange for your middle name, I'll open your mind to the ideas of the Universe. But you'll never remember what it was that came after Larry, but before Plum. And you won't remember me until you're much too old to come back and disturb my meditations. Do you agree?'

'It's a deal,' he chirped, staring up at me.

'Then come here little man,' I said, extended an open hand.

"He shook it, and suddenly his eyes began to whirl, and I could see the ideas of the world rushing into his mind. As he turned to go, I had to remind him. 'Aren't you forgetting something, Master Plum?'

'Oh yeah.'

"He trotted back to me, and whispered his middle name into my ear. 'An excellent name,' I said, as I absorbed it deeply into recesses of my already-much-too-long ancient Buddhist mantric name. When it was all done, he smiled at me—outwardly the same boy, but with something a little different in his eyes. There was a gleam—the same gleam that came into my eyes when I was just the boy Buddha. He ran for the opening of my cave. Just when he reached the jade archway to my home, which some have called the Eighth wonder of the world, I heard him call out.

The Idea Man

'Good-bye, Budd! Thank you for everything! And don't forget to get out and enjoy the sky and the water from time to time. Just because you know when they began and what they ultimately mean doesn't mean you can't play in them!'

"And when he was gone, this young Larry Plum, with his opened mind and an innocent heart, I couldn't but laugh long and hard about the little boy who had breezed into my day, interrupted my mantra, and left as an Idea Man. And for the first time in many years—how many I can't even remember—I took a break from my meditations, and went out for a long walk underneath the sky."

I looked over at Plum, who was nodding the nod of recollection. Everything had all come back to him seventy-two years after the deal was made—everything but the name itself.

"So what do you say, Budd? How about giving me back my middle name? Don't you think I've been without it long enough?"

He smiled at the Buddha, and I sensed that two mind-full warriors were about to do battle once more.

"And why should I do that, Plum? Why should I give you your middle name back? You've had an open mind for an entire lifetime, and besides, I like your middle name—always have. No, I think I'm going to keep it."

And he smiled.

A negotiating session of mythic proportions then broke out. I'm betting there's never been anything on this Earth to match it. Plum offered up one idea after another that he had come up with over the years, offering to trade with the Buddha for his middle name.

"Surely this will interest you," Plum said, "the secret to catharsis—"

"Already know it," Buddha replied, "and it only takes ninety-four minutes."

"How about why some trees live one thousand years but never speak except to the wind."

"Not interested."

I was, though I wouldn't have dreamt of interrupting this exchange.

"The mystery of friendship?" Plum said with raised eyebrows.

"Good try, but you're too late Plum. I got that one straight three years back, otherwise I might have been interested."

"OK, how about what happened to the dinosaurs in the Pleistocene?"

"Alien exodus to the Kartus galaxy—an astounding undertaking, I hear. They got them out about a month before the meteor hit."

It went on like this for hours. Plum would offer up some amazing idea, many of which even I had never heard before, courtesy in part of the open mind Budd had given him in return for his middle name. Then Budd would summarily reject the offer. He either knew the answer already, or it wasn't a big enough deal for him to give up what had become his favorite prize.

When they claimed the same discovery, a good-natured battle would break out over this or that fine point. Does meaning really depend on the soul or does it exist on its own? Was the platypus a paradigm anomaly or just an ugly beaver-outcast-screw-up? They laughed and shouted at one another, and I realized what was happening. Two great minds had come together for one last hurrah—playing like boys do, only with the ideas of the Universe.

But ultimately none of Plum's ideas were acceptable for his middle name. All three of us were exhausted, and it was time to go home.

"So there's nothing, Budd, that I can give you to get my middle name back? Nothing I can think of, nothing you can think of, nothing in this Universe or any other to make you change your mind?"

"I'm sorry Plum. It's been great fun, but I can't think of anything at all," Budd said to his old friend, "I can't just give it away. I couldn't sleep with myself if I did. It's got to be a fair trade, or no trade at all. We can't go throwing the Universe out of balance, can we?"

To this day, I'm not sure why something welled up from deep in my belly, raced through my esophagus, and blasted out of my mouth, "How about my middle name! Yes—take my middle name and give back Plum's. What could be more balanced? A name for a name!"

The room was silent. Plum looked at me with that smile of friendship that few people are lucky enough to share in their lifetime. Then he walked over and put his arm around me.

"Let's go, Boy. It's been quite a day—yes, quite a day."

And we walked together, shoulder to shoulder out of the sacred chamber of the Buddha.

But just as we were about to emerge from Budd's cave and back into the daylight, now with its final rays of sunlight faltering in the heavy dusk, a sound broke from the cavern.

"Deal! Boy's middle name for Plum's, straight up."

Now Buddha was standing at the opening of his cave, right beneath the magical jade arch.

"Don't do it, old Boy," Plum said, trying in vain to stop me from doing what he would have done for me in an instant.

I stepped up to the Buddha, and whispered my middle name into his ear. He nodded.

"Not bad, Boy, not bad!" And then my mind began to whirl.

He smiled and had turned back inside when I reminded him. "Aren't you forgetting something?"

"Oh yeah," he said. Then he approached Plum and put his mouth to Plum's right ear.

"You're kidding me!" Plum laughed hysterically.

"I know! Isn't that something!" Budd said, staring Plum in the face before turning his eyes back to me. "Who would have guessed!"

Then Budd shook both of our hands.

"Maybe I'll see you two Boys again someday. Don't be strangers. That's no good for anyone!"

He turned and disappeared into the darkness.

It was a long quiet walk back to the outskirts of the village, the dramatic sunset of vibrant color leading the way. We didn't talk, but when we reached our hut, Plum turned to me.

"Thank you, Boy."

"For what, Plum?"

"For everything. Thank you for this life and the last, thank you for this friendship and for my name—thank you for all of it."

"Don't mention it."

I smiled at my best friend. But I also thought to myself, 'Why on earth is he thanking me for his name? Has he lost his mind?'

I didn't remember a thing.

24. The End

In the end we grew ancient together, Plum and I—well into our nineties. Nothing about us changed much. Perhaps the adventures took place a little closer to home. But there were still new adventures and stories to tell for those years, which says something about a pair of nonagenarians.

Whenever the two of us landed in trouble, it just meant there were more people still shaking their heads, and trying to explain to the people of Seasoncreek why Old Boy deserved another chance. Consider for example the Shlagenhoff Fiasco.

On my ninety-fourth birthday I was strolling down Main Street, eating an Italian ice—first discovered in Poland, if you want to know the truth, but "Polish ice" never caught on. Plum spotted me, and paying no mind to crosswalks, signals or signs, he made a direct line for me.

"Boy," he hollered, "I've got something big in mind—"

I turned, and right at that moment I heard the awful-horrible screech of brakes-against-metal-and-rubber-on-street.

Seasoncreek's overzealous and foul mouthed law enforcer, Officer Shlagenhoff, who enforced all and any of Seasoncreek's laws without ever paying mind to reason or sense, had nearly flattened me with his police car, bringing its bumper right up against, but not over, my aged body. Plum disappeared from my line of sight as I collapsed under the car. That bully of a policeman leapt from the vehicle to see what remained of this old man whom he had always disliked—though he disliked almost everyone. A crowd began to form, and so did a great commotion.

By the time Plum got to the presumed carnage—it took him a long time now to cover the fifty yards that separated us—he was really afraid that it would be too late so say goodbye. With his brass-knobbed cane in one hand, and a large Italian ice of his own in the other, he passed through the circle of onlookers. Seconds later, Shlagenhoff was lying in Plum's shadow in a pool of my melting Italian ice, holding his right knee, writhing in pain, and screaming bloody murder.

"What's happened?" I asked, somewhat bewildered.

"This old bastard has knee-capped me!" The policeman screamed to the crowd, trying to stand again on his one good leg.

"Oh, is that how it is, Shlagenhoff?" I replied. "It's always so black and white with you law enforcement types. Why don't you tell the good people why you took one for the team, before I give you another!"

Before the conversation degenerated any further into personal attacks, excuses, and slander, I asked the crowd for an account of what had happened.

As I now understand it, when I saw my friend, I stepped carelessly into the middle of the street. Shlagenhoff was bearing down on me in his car, but he didn't see me, because his eyes were fixed on a chocolate eclair he had just purchased from the Ultimate Pastry Shop. When he did look up, he reacted, and his brakes brought him to a halt one eighth of an inch from my body. But his hood ornament had dashed the fabulous Italian (Polish) ice in my left hand.

The officer had jumped out of his car, and yelled.

"You Old Coot! Be more damned careful crossing the street, or I will run you over the next time, and you'll deserve it!'

To which Plum apparently replied, "Watch your language, and your meanness. There are children around here, and I won't have them exposed to either."

Shlagenhoff replied that he would say what he wanted to any 'old bastard,' and in front of anyone he 'bloody well pleased.' Plum disagreed, and he also demanded reparations for my lost Polish-Italian ice. Shlangenhoff refused, and the fact that he cursed for a third time, with five year old Stevie Piker standing right there, so outraged Plum that he struck Shlagenhoff's right knee with a precise brass-cane-suprapatellar-blow, sending him to the ground right in the puddle of my fast melting shaved ice.

To my recollection, the officer and Plum had to be separated. We had never been much as fighters, and we certainly weren't at ninety-four, in spite of our wiry builds. But my old friend really wanted another piece of Shlagenhoff, who called for back up. The rest of Seasoncreek's police force soon arrived on the scene—all four of them.

"Arrest that man!" a red-faced, enraged, and humiliated Shlagenhoff screamed. "Arrest him and take him away!"

The other policemen couldn't settle him down. I worried that this overweight eclair-eating-lunatic was going to have a stroke. By then a very large crowd had gathered to witness the commotion that Larry Plum had caused.

"On what grounds, may I ask, do you intend to make this arrest?" I asked.

"Well...maybe...perhaps..." Shlagenhoff stammered, still holding onto his fast swelling knee, "Jaywalking!" he finally blurted out, and I was slapped into handcuffs, and taken away.

Plum bailed me out two hours later from Seasoncreek's one cell police station. I could have left immediately, but he liked the idea of getting some time to torture the police with some of his ideas on the judicial system and its inadequacies. By the time I did post bail they were begging me to leave. They couldn't stand another exposition on the first amendment, the right to a speedy and fair trial, and proper representation. By the time I left, they had even fully reimbursed me for the lost Polish ice!

"You know, Boy, doing time has given many a man time to think."

"Plum, I was only in jail for one hundred and twenty-two minutes!"

"Ah, yes," he said, smiling his classic Plum smile, with the gleam in his eye, "but catharsis only takes ninety-four."

"Is that what this was about Plum? Catharsis? Shlagenhoff? Prison?"

"Maybe. I'm glad you're out."

"Me too."

We walked home, but not before stopping for an ethnic frozen dessert to replace the one I had lost.

And so we went on, still at odds with authority figures, eating Polish ice, remembering adventures from the past and creating adventures anew—never slowing down. Each night we retired to my office to reflect on the newest idea to emerge from the Idea Man's mind.

"Boy!"

"Yes, Plum," I answered, not looking up from my newspaper.

"Dying is a lot like living—only with less breathing."

I looked up. Plum was taking slow, deep, and deliberate breaths, almost as if someone was sitting on his chest. His eyes were glazed full moons, looking off toward the stars.

"My God, what's wrong, Plum?"

I was soon at his side.

"Oh I'm just dying, Boy," he said softly. His eyes refocused on me, but breathing was becoming even more labored.

"Why didn't you tell me something was wrong!"

The doctor in me was rearing his ugly head.

"Because there's nothing wrong with dying, Boy."

I knew he was right. There really wasn't anything wrong with dying. Not this way. Not at this time of life. Not with your best friend at your side.

"Boy, I want to tell you something I've been thinking about quite a lot lately."

"What's that, Plum?" I said, frightened.

"The secret of life, Boy, the secret of life."

"Oh is that all you've been thinking about? Why don't you hold off on dying for a while, and tell me when you feel better."

"I don't feel bad," he said slowly. "The secret of life is your friendships. And it's really no secret at all. Just have them."

"What Plum?"

"Have friendships. That's the secret! It's all we need."

And it was certainly all the two of us had ever needed—an Idea Man and his best friend. We were together, as we had always really been, here at Plum's end.

His breaths came more slowly, and as a doctor, I knew his end was near. I had seen many deaths, but never had one felt like this one. I felt Plum's passing, as surely as I felt the warm passage of tears down my cheeks.

"What are you doing Boy?" Plum said, with a strange re-found energy and strength. "Stop that crying! Forests and streams are forever—we're not. Ninety-five years? It's obscene—only sea turtles should live this long. And besides the closest thing to any end in this circular universe is the beginning!"

He chuckled, and closed his eyes.

"What do you mean Plum?"

I really wanted to ask him "What does it all mean?"

There was a long pause in his breathing, and then, just when I was ready to let him go, my old friend spoke again.

"Everything, Boy. It meant everything. Remember everything that we've done together, and you'll never be alone."

The Idea Man

What happened then is a bit confusing to me even now. In the seconds after Plum died a wave of emotion washed over me, intense as a thunderstorm over the sea. I struggled to hold onto life myself, and some of my own energy escaped into the air around us. I was angry that he was gone, angry that I was alone. I struck him hard on the chest—so hard that I felt the ground shake beneath us (later I learned that Seasoncreek experienced its first earthquake in ninety-five years at that moment—I guess that weather is emotion after all.

That blow, I swore, awoke the sleeper, and Plum's eyes opened one last time—eyes bright as they were in his youth.

"Well, Boy, now I've seen it all!"

His voice was young and strong.

"What, Plum? What did you see?"

"All of it!"

And he passed smiling into the next adventure.

24. Beginning Again

My family and I had just moved into new town called Seasoncreek, and because school was out, my parents sent me off to the local baseball field so that I could meet other kids. I was very anxious—and not just because I had no friends yet. I was also a weak baseball player and this was the last thing that I wanted an intimidating bunch of five, six, and seven year olds to know about me first.

I was actually a passable fielder, with a half-decent arm and a flare for the dramatic catch. But I couldn't hit the ball a lick, and there's nothing like a strikeout to put the new kid on the bench for the summer, and maybe a lifetime.

I prayed to be sent to the outfield, and amazingly, the call came. I trotted out, wearing my new black-and-gold Pittsburgh Pirates baseball cap.

The players taunted each other, and the tiny pitcher dug away at the mound with his sneakers. Out in center field, the sky was a striking blue, with a lone cloud beginning to form above me. Slowly, it took on a outline, and then a shape—that of a ripe Plum, with a purplish tinge at the edges.

The Idea Man

As I stared up at this cloud, I felt a sensation that I have never forgotten—though perhaps I have forgotten almost everything else. My hat began to squeeze tightly around my skull, almost as if my head was growing larger by the second. The cloud grew larger too, and it hovered above me.

A violent crack of the bat, and the sparkling new Spalding baseball my father had tossed to me an hour before flew into the blinding sun and deep into centerfield. I tracked the fly as it soared higher and farther than any six-year old boy could hit it. I sprinted for the fence at the far end of our ballpark. My cap tightened another notch, squeezing my brains deeper into my body. As I reached up to make the greatest catch of my life, the baseball disappeared into the Plum-shaped cloud and was never seen again.

25. The End Again

"What is that boy doing in center field?" a wiry old man sitting on a hill, watching the baseball game asked.

"Why does anyone do anything?" the large bald man sitting cross-legged beside him answered.

"He's been rolling around out there for at least two minutes. It looks like he's trying to get that hat off of his head."

"It's a big head, isn't it?"

"Yes, too big!"

"But full of ideas, perhaps?"

It was.

26. Plumisms

A person's head grows exactly two sizes bigger when an idea of any importance comes into it.

It never hurts to get away as long as you don't leave yourself behind!

Your best friend is the person you never mind seeing.

Nothing's really a matter of life or death unless you're actually dying!

A younger brother is an excellent thing to have; he's bound to make you seem responsible.

Things are never black or white . . . unless they're red.

Pride is a disease, and asparagus is the cure!

Money, unlike water, runs upstream—and luckily you can still drown in it!

Organ removal is the wave of the future!

When it comes to the opposite sex, forget your brain and follow your guts. They will lead you to love every time.

When you see your dreams up too close they tend to fly away.

Anyone who tells you to be on time has some problem or another, probably psychological.

Finding one's middle name always takes precedence over work.

It's terrifying to search for yourself; you never know what you might not find.

The secret of life is your friendships. And it's really no secret at all—just have them!

Discovery comes in the strangest places—usually where you're least likely to look, but often in a friend's face.

Never forget, breathing is an important part of life, but it's not automatic.

Looking back now, it wasn't a mistake then.

About The Artist

Krystal Tavares, an early childhood educator, has been drawing ever since her 16th Christmas, when she found colored pencils in her stocking. She lives in Millilani, Hawai'i with her husband and brother.

Also from Lō'ihi Press

Hawai'i Smiles by Robert Barclay

A collection of eight light-hearted short stories for the local Hawai'i audience interested in easy reading and laugh-out-loud humor. Settings and characters will be familiar, while fresh and original plots and circumstances break into new literary territory. Tourists might also enjoy this comic and heart-warming perspective on life in Hawai'i, which will strike a chord with their own unique sense of home and place.

Coming Soon

In The Time Before Light by Ian MacMillan

A novel of Hawai'i history and worldly adventure, from one of Hawaii's most outstanding storytellers.

Yakudoshi by Stacy Fukuhara.

When Police Sergeant Brent Oyadamori faces his 41st birthday, a hilarious cataclysm of events ensues as he tries to buy, beg, borrow, and steal his family the perfect home he believes they deserve.

THE IDEA MAN

A Novel of Adventure, Friendship, and the Secret of Life

For Cousin Judy!

With love,

Joel